'Do I collect have a partne Miss Filmer?'

To Athene's great surprise Nicholas Cameron bowed in her direction. 'If so I would be honoured to take you on to the floor.'

Athene offered him a small bow. 'It would be my pleasure, too, sir.'

This statement was not entirely untruthful. Something about Nick Cameron frightened her, but she could not, in decency, refuse him, and if she were honest she was beginning to find him strangely attractive. Besides, it was, after all, a kind offer, for no one would have expected him to squire an insignificant companion.

He was holding his hand out to her.

She took it.

Immediately the strong sensation which had surprised them before surprised them again. Nick, stifling his own rapid response, led Athene towards the opposite side of the room where a number of couples were assembling for the dance.

A young woman disappears.
A husband is suspected of murder.
Stirring times for all the neighbourhood in

The STEEPWOOD
Scandal

Book 8

When the debauched Marquis of Sywell won
Steepwood Abbey years ago at cards, it led to the death
of the then Earl of Yardley. Now he's caused scandal
again by marrying a girl out of his class—and young
enough to be his granddaughter! After being married
only a short time, the Marchioness has disappeared,
leaving no trace of her whereabouts. There is every
expectation that yet more scandals will emerge, though
no one yet knows just how shocking they will be.

The four villages surrounding the Steepwood Abbey
estate are in turmoil, not only with the dire goings-on
at the Abbey, but also with their own affairs. Each
story in **The Steepwood Scandal** follows the mystery
behind the disappearance of the young woman, and the
individual romances of lovers connected in some way
with the intrigue.

Regency Drama
intrigue, mischief...and marriage

AN UNCONVENTIONAL DUENNA

Paula Marshall

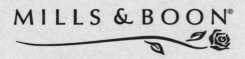
MILLS & BOON®

All the characters in this book have no existence outside the imagination of the author, and have no relation whatsoever to anyone bearing the same name or names. They are not even distantly inspired by any individual known or unknown to the author, and all the incidents are pure invention.

*First published in Great Britain 2001
Harlequin Mills & Boon Limited,
Eton House, 18-24 Paradise Road, Richmond, Surrey TW9 1SR*

© Harlequin Books S.A. 2001

Special thanks and acknowledgement are given to Paula Marshall for her contribution to The Steepwood Scandal series.

ISBN 0 263 82849 2

*Set in Times Roman 10½ on 12½ pt.
119-1201-57905*

*Printed and bound in Spain
by Litografia Rosés S.A., Barcelona*

Paula Marshall, married with three children, has had a varied life. She began her career in a large library and ended it as a university academic in charge of History. She has travelled widely, has been a swimming coach, and has appeared on *University Challenge* and *Mastermind*. She has always wanted to write, and likes her novels to be full of adventure and humour.

Look out for
THE MISSING MARCHIONESS
by Paula Marshall

in **The Steepwood Scandal**
Coming soon

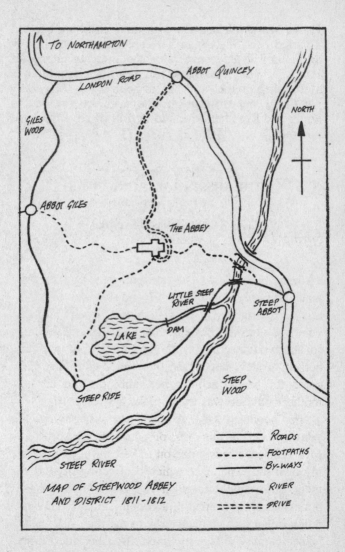

TO NORTHAMPTON

LONDON ROAD

ABBOT QUINCEY

GILES WOOD

NORTH

ABBOT GILES

THE ABBEY

LITTLE STEEP RIVER

STEEP ABBOT

DAM

LAKE

STEEP WOOD

STEEP RIDE

STEEP RIVER

ROADS
FOOTPATHS
BY-WAYS
RIVER
DRIVE

MAP OF STEEPWOOD ABBEY
AND DISTRICT 1811 - 1812

PROLOGUE

Spring 1812

Athene Filmer, twenty years old, poor and illegitimate, had only one aim in life and that was to make a good marriage. She fully intended to marry a man who was not only rich but also had a title. By doing so she would settle her mother for life as well as herself. Today, out of the blue, an opportunity had come for her to achieve her ambition and all her mother could do was try to make her reject it!

'For goodness sake, Athene,' she was saying, 'if you must accept this offer of a London Season from Mrs Tenison, I must beg you to be careful. It may be my own sad experience which is affecting my judgement, but I should not wish you to end up as I have done—a lonely woman in a country village. I would much rather that you stayed with me than risk that.'

The country village to which Mrs Charlotte Filmer

referred was Steep Ride, where she and her daughter lived in what was little more than a cottage, ambitiously called Datchet House. Steep Ride was pleasantly situated in the wooded neighbourhood of Steepwood Abbey, not far from the River Steep and its tributary which ran through the Abbey grounds.

Mrs Filmer was, not without reason, looking anxiously at her daughter. Alas, Athene was not only clever, but she was also determined and wilful—one might almost call her headstrong! In that she was the opposite of her mother, who was gentle and retiring, and whose one lapse from the straight and narrow path of virtue had been cruelly punished. In her first and only Season the young man whom she had loved had betrayed her, and though she called herself Mrs she had never been married. Her one consolation lay in her pride in her beautiful child.

'Dear Mama,' said Athene, leaning forward affectionately and kissing her anxious parent, 'I shall only be going as a mixture of a companion and a friend for my dear old schoolfellow, Emma. You may be sure that Mrs Tenison will keep a firm eye on both of us. Depend upon it, she will not allow me to outshine Emma, since her intention is to secure a good match for her.'

'She will have no trouble doing that,' fretted Mrs Filmer. 'What I do not understand is why she isn't engaging some decent, middle-aged woman to look after her rather than trying to persuade you to be her companion. After all, you are not very much older than Emma and might be considered to need a guardian or a chaperon yourself.'

'Now, Mama, you know as well as I do what a timid little thing Emma is. The sort of dragon you are describing would extinguish her, whereas I am her good friend and guardian from her school-days who protected her when she needed protection. I am also old enough for her to look up to me, but not so ancient and stern that I frighten her. I shall stand between her and the Tenisons' sponsor, Lady Dunlop, who is somewhat of a dragon. Besides, would you deprive me of the delights of a London Season because you were unfortunate? You were young and inexperienced in the ways of the world, whereas I have had the benefit for the last few years of being made aware by you of the traps which await the innocent in the often cruel world of the ton.'

'There is that,' sighed her mother. 'Nevertheless...'

'Nevertheless nothing,' said Athene firmly. She had the advantage of always having won her arguments with her mother in the past. Her own internal reaction when Mrs Tenison had called earlier that afternoon with her exciting proposal had been: At last! Here is the chance I have always wished for—and so soon, before I have reached my last prayers.

'You might not wish to take up this offer, my dear, once you have thought it over. You will, in effect, be one of the Tenisons' servants, little better than a governess. You will be kept in the background. I know that Mrs Tenison said that she would provide you with a suitable wardrobe, but you may be sure that it will not be either becoming or fashionable. I am sure that she will not want you to rival Emma…'

'Now, how could I do that,' wondered Athene, 'when Emma is all that is fashionable and I am not. She is blonde, blue-eyed and tiny, whereas I am dark, grey-eyed and tall—an unlikely sort of creature to attract the young bucks of the ton.'

Her mother forbore to say that Athene always caused heads to turn at the dances at the Assembly Rooms in Abbot Quincey and was already noted for her wit and address, even if her hair and her grey eyes were the wrong colour and her turn-outs far from being in the latest fashion. It would not do to over-praise her: she thought quite enough of herself as it was.

Instead she offered in as neutral a voice as she could, 'I still think that you should give this whole notion more thought than you are doing. For one thing, if anyone should learn—or suspect—that you are illegitimate you will be ruined.'

Athene tossed her head. 'I'll think about it again tonight, Mama, and tell you in the morning what my decision is.'

She had no intention of doing any such thing. Her mind was already made up. Here was her chance. Somehow, however much Mrs Tenison tried to extinguish her, she would make her mark in London society and hook her rich and titled fish. She remembered one of the older girls saying that immediately before she left Mrs Guarding's school to go to

London for the Season. She had certainly managed to hook *her* fish: a baronet—admittedly not of the first stare—but a fish with a title nonetheless.

An irreverent Athene had once wondered how much like a fish he *had* looked. Was he a shark—or a simple-seeming goggle-eyed cod? She hoped that her fish would be handsome, good and kind as well as rich and titled—which might be asking rather a lot, but one ought always to aim for the highest…

Naturally she would not allow either her mother or Mrs Tenison to guess at her true reason for accepting this somewhat surprising offer: she would be as good and demure and grateful as a poor young lady could be. Consequently, when they were both invited to the Tenisons' to be informed of the details of her employment, Mrs Tenison thought that Miss Athene Filmer had gained a quite undeserved reputation for being outspoken and downright in her manner.

Emma, of course, was delighted. Her face shone with pleasure when Athene and her mother were shown into the Tenisons' drawing-room, and for once she acted impulsively.

'Oh, Athene!' she exclaimed, running forward to take her friend's hand. 'You cannot know how pleased I am that you have agreed to come with us! I shall not feel frightened of anything if you are standing by my side!'

'Come, come, Miss Tenison,' said her mother coldly, 'that is no way to behave. Thank your friend quietly and in a proper fashion. Remember also that she is to be your companion, almost a chaperon, not your bosom bow, so you will address her as Miss Filmer. You, and only you, are to be presented to the Prince Regent. I trust that you understand what your proper place will be, Miss Filmer?'

Athene bowed submissively. 'Oh, indeed, Mrs Tenison. I am to accompany Miss Emma as her support, not her equal in any way.'

'But I shall allow you to call me Emma in private,' exclaimed her daughter eagerly. 'After all, we were friends at school, were we not?'

'True,' said Mrs Tenison, still cold, 'but you will not refer to that fact in public. I have called this meeting today in order to inform Miss Filmer of her duties, and to make arrangements for her wardrobe to be made in the village before we leave. You, Emma, will have a small number of dresses run up in Northampton, but your best toilettes will be ordered from a London *modiste* when we reach there.'

It was quite plain, thought Athene, that Mrs Tenison intended her to have no illusions about the humble nature of her post in London. This judgement was immediately reinforced when Mrs Tenison added, 'If you have any reservations about accepting my offer, Miss Filmer, pray raise them now. We must not start out on a false note.'

'No, indeed, Mrs Tenison,' agreed Athene, dodging her mother's rueful glances in her direction, while Mrs Tenison continued to reinforce her subordinate position. 'I quite understand the terms of my employment.'

'I hope you also understand,' said Mrs Tenison, 'that other than providing you with suitable clothing and bed and board, I am not offering you any money for your services. Your reward is to visit London in the height of the Season as the companion of a young lady of good family.'

She did not, thought Athene cynically, refer to her daughter as an heiress. An heiress who was looking for a husband with a fortune and a title. While the Tenisons were not enormously rich, Emma would be inheriting £15,000, enough to attract at least a baronet—or a Viscount if she were lucky. She also had the possibility of inheriting further wealth from a maiden aunt.

Without waiting for an answer Mrs Tenison turned to Mrs Filmer. 'I trust that you, too, madam, are happy with the splendid opportunity which I am offering your daughter.'

That gentle lady cast another agonised glance at Athene. She was as charmingly pretty and withdrawn as Mrs Tenison was handsome and forthright. A stranger to the room would have thought that Emma was her daughter and Athene Mrs Tenison's.

Of course, she was not happy—but how could she tell Mrs Tenison that? For was not Athene's patron the leader of local society in the village of Steep Ride, whose word was law, who had the ear of the parson at Abbot Quincey and the assorted nobility and gentry of the district around Steepwood?

'If that is what Athene wishes…' she began hesitantly.

'Then that's settled,' said Mrs Tenison loudly and sweepingly taking poor Mrs Filmer's reply for granted.

She rang the bell with great vigour and demanded the tea board of the servant who answered. She had heard that some members of the fashionable world had been drinking tea in the afternoon instead of after dinner and had decided to lead the fashion as well.

No need to allow her two humble dependants to know how much it pleased her to have gained a companion on the cheap while appearing to be conferring a favour on them!

'Truly remarkable, m'lord!' enthused Hemmings, the valet of Adrian Drummond, Lord Kinloch. 'Between us we have achieved a *nonpareil!*'

He was referring to his employer's cravat which, after several perilous minutes, he had managed to tie in one of the latest modes. Adrian, not sure that he was totally satisfied with Hemmings's masterpiece, swung round to show it off to his cousin, Nick Cameron, who was seated in an armchair, watching the pantomime which Adrian made of preparing himself for the day.

'What do you think, Nick?' he asked anxiously. 'Will it do?'

If Adrian was tricked out almost beyond current fashion in his desire to be recognised as one of London society's greatest pinks, Nick showed his contempt for such frivolities by dressing as casually as though he were back at home in the Highlands of Scotland—a country which Adrian had not visited for many years.

'Who,' Adrian always declaimed theatrically when asked why he had never returned to his family's place of origin since he had left it when little more than a boy, 'would wish to be stranded in such a wilderness?'

Now Nick put his head on one side and said in a voice as considered as though he were being asked a serious question about the current state of the war in Europe, 'Do you really want my honest opinion, Adrian?'

'Indeed, Nick. I would value it.'

'Then I wonder why you spend so much of your time worrying about the exact way in which a large piece of cloth is arranged around your neck. Would not a simple bow suffice? And also save you a great deal of heartache.'

Adrian said stiffly, for once reminding Nick of the difference in their social standing, 'It is all very well for you to ignore the dictates of society, but I have a position to keep up. It would not do for *me* to go around dressed like a gamekeeper.'

'I scarcely look like one,' murmured Nick, examining his perfectly respectable, if somewhat dull, navy-blue breeches, coat, simple cravat and shining boots from Lobbs. 'But I do take your point. The Earl of Kinloch must present himself as the very maypole of fashion.'

There had been a time when the two young men had been boys together when such a set-down from Nick would have had them rolling on the ground in an impromptu battle: Adrian struggling to make Nick take back the implied insult and Nick striving to justify it. Afterwards they would rise, shake hands and remain friends. Nick had a bottom of good sense which Adrian always, if dimly, respected and on many occasions had saved the pair of them from the wrath of their seniors.

Hemmings said helpfully, 'I think, m'lord, that a little tweak to the left would improve what might already be seen as satisfactory, but which would make it superb. Allow me.'

Adrian turned round; Hemmings duly tweaked. Adrian, admiring the result in the mirror, said to Nick, 'There, that is exactly the sort of adjustment which I was asking you to supply. A fellow cannot really see it for himself—he takes his own appearance for granted.'

'True,' said Nick lazily. 'May I ask why you are so bent on displaying yourself to your best advantage today?'

'I'm driving us to Hyde Park, of course. There, one must be seen to be caring of one's appearance, as you would allow, I am sure.'

'We have been to the park before, but seldom after such a brouhaha. May one know why?'

Adrian signalled to Hemmings that, his work over, he might leave, and came and sat opposite his cousin. This was a somewhat difficult feat since he chose to wear his breeches so tightly cut that sitting down became almost perilous. On the other hand the breeches showed off a pair of splendid legs—the whole point of the exercise.

'The truth is,' he said, 'that my mother has been besieging me again about marriage. She is becoming so wearisome on the subject that I fear that I must give way and oblige her. She does have a point in that I am the last of the Kinlochs and when I pop off there will be no one left to assume the title if I don't oblige. I intend to look over all the available heiresses who possess some sort of beauty. I couldn't marry an ugly woman, however rich, because if I did I shouldn't be able to oblige Mama over the business of offspring. My wife must be as attractive as my dear Kitty. A pity that I can't marry *her*—no difficulty about offspring, then.'

'My dear Kitty' was Adrian's ladybird, whom he had set up in rooms in the fashionable end of Chelsea and to whom he was as loyal as though she were his wife. A great deal more loyal, in fact, than many members of the aristocracy were to their legitimate wives.

'Mmm,' said Nick gravely, suppressing a desire to laugh at this artless confession. 'I do see your point.

Very well, I will come with you and help you to make a list of all those young ladies whom you might consider eligible.'

'Excellent!' exclaimed Adrian. 'I knew that you would be able to assist me if you put your mind to it.'

He rose. 'Tallyho and taratantara! Let's make a start, then. The sooner I find a wife the sooner Mama will cease to badger me.'

'I would point out,' offered Nick, slipping an arm through his cousin's, 'that the Season has barely started and all the new beauties who will be on offer have not yet arrived. I shouldn't be too hasty, if I were you.'

'There is that,' agreed Adrian happily. 'Besides, what about you, Nick? Shall you join me in this exercise? I know that your parents never badger you about providing Strathdene Castle with an heir, but you really should, you know. After all, it's years since that wretched business with Flora Campbell—time to forget it. Perhaps I could badger you. It's time I badgered you about something. You have had your own way with me for far too long.'

'Badger away,' said Nick easily, refusing to rise to Adrian's comment about Flora. 'I am quite happy to remain single. I've never yet met the woman I would care to live with—or whom I could trust—but who knows, this Season might be different.'

He didn't really believe what he was saying. 'That wretched business with Flora Campbell' had inevitably, and permanently, coloured all his feelings about women of every class, but it would not do to tell Adrian that. What he would do was look after Adrian now that the inevitable fortune-hunters were circling round to secure him as a husband for their daughters.

All in all they were as unalike as two men could be. Nick was dark, dour, clever and cynical; Adrian was bright, fair, trusting and relatively simple-minded. Their only resemblance lay in their height: they were both tall. Adrian had once said in a rare fit of understanding, 'If I were King, I'd appoint you Prime Minister, Nick. We'd make a rare team.'

So they would, Nick had thought. They were closer than brothers and nothing had yet come between them. Now, he slipped an arm through Adrian's and they walked to the stables where Adrian's new and splendid two-horse curricle was waiting.

CHAPTER ONE

'For goodness sake, Emma, do stand up straight,' hissed Mrs Tenison at her daughter. 'Do not hang your head. Take Athene as your model. She at least is aware of the proper carriage of a gentlewoman.'

'I'll try, Mama,' faltered Emma, 'but you know how much I dislike crowds.'

'Enough of such whim-whams,' commanded Mrs Tenison severely. 'Be ready to curtsey to your hostess when you reach the top of the stairs. And you, Athene, remember to stand a little to our rear and refrain from drawing attention to yourself.'

'Of course, Mrs Tenison,' said Athene submissively.

They were at Lady Leominster's ball which, although it was always held in mid-April, was the first truly grand event of the Season when everyone who was anyone had finally arrived in London, and everyone who was anyone would be present at it. The Tenisons had previously attended, under the wing of

Lady Dunlop, who accompanied them everywhere, several minor functions where they had met no one of any consequence and all of the young gentlemen present appeared to be already married.

Emma was looking modestly charming, but provincial, in her pale pink gauze dress, made in Northampton. She was wearing on her blonde curls a wreath of red silk rosebuds nestling amid their pale green leaves. Her jewellery was modest: a pearl necklace and two small pendant pearl earrings. Mrs Tenison possessed enough good sense to realise that the famous Tenison parure made up of large emeralds surrounded by diamonds would have appeared garish if worn by her delicate-looking daughter. The misery of it was that they would merely have served to enhance Athene's looks had she been entitled to wear them.

She had also made sure that Athene would not diminish Emma by having her attired in a dark grey, high-necked silk dress of even more antique cut than Emma's. Finally to extinguish her, as though she were an over-bright candle which needed snuffing, Athene had been made to wear a large linen and lace duenna's cap which covered her beautiful dark hair and hid half of her face. As a final gesture to remind Athene of her subordinate position, her hair had been scraped so tightly back from her face, and bound so severely, that its deep waves had disappeared and would not have been seen even without the ugly cap.

Athene had borne all this with patience, since it

was the only way in which she would ever be able to attend anything half so grand as the Leominsters' ball. Her party was surrounded by all the greatest names in the land on their long and slow walk up the grand staircase. Mr and Mrs Tenison had already spoken to several cousins, including their most grand relative of all, the Marquis of Exford.

Athene liked Mr Tenison. Unlike his wife he always spoke to her kindly, and when he had found her reading in the library of his London house shortly after they had arrived in town he had been pleased to discover that, unlike Emma and Mrs Tenison, she had a genuine interest in its contents.

He had taken to advising her on what to read, and had provided her with a book-list of recommended texts. On those afternoons when Emma and her mother visited friends and relatives, leaving Athene behind, since her guardianship and support was not needed on these minor social occasions, he enjoyed listening to her opinion of her latest excursion into the world of learning. He had already discovered that she had a good grasp of Latin and had lamented to him that ladies were not supposed to learn Greek.

Today, when they had been alone together in the drawing-room before the Tenisons had set off for Leominster House in Piccadilly he had said, 'Good gracious, my dear Miss Filmer. Is there really any need for you to wear anything quite so disfiguring as your present get-up?'

Athene had lowered her eyes. She had no wish to

provoke the unnecessary battle which would follow any attempt at intervention on her behalf by Mr Tenison. More than that, she was already aware that he always lost such encounters. Worldly wisdom also told her that Mrs Tenison might become suspicious of her husband's intentions towards her if he chose to become too openly friendly with the unconsidered Miss Filmer.

'It is important,' she said quietly, 'that I do not attempt to outshine my dear little Emma in any way, nor lead any gentleman to imagine that I am present in London in order to look for a husband, since I have no dowry. My duty is to look after her and give her the courage to enjoy herself in a crowded room. You must know how distressed she becomes whenever she is in a crowd.'

He had nodded mournfully at her. 'Yes, I am well aware of why my wife has asked you to accompany us, but I cannot say that I quite approve of you being made to look twice your age.'

'That is part of the bargain to which I agreed,' said Athene, astonished at her own duplicity and at her ability to play the humble servant so successfully. 'I beg of you not to trouble yourself on my account.'

'So be it, if that is what you wish,' he had said, and his wife's entrance, towing along a reluctant Emma who was suffering from a severe case of stage-fright at the prospect of being among so many famous people, had put an end to the conversation.

Now, looking around the huge ballroom, aglow

with light from a myriad of chandeliers beneath which splendidly dressed men and women talked, walked and danced, Athene felt like the man in the old story who said that the most amazing thing about the room in which he found himself was that he was in it.

Stationed as she was, standing behind the Tenisons, who were of course, all seated, she wondered distractedly how she was to begin her own campaign. It was going to be much more difficult than she had imagined. No doubt in his early days Napoleon Bonaparte himself must have had such thoughts, but look where he had ended up—as Emperor of France!

Well, her ambition was not so grand as his, and she would be but a poor thing if she made no efforts to attain it. Perhaps in the end it would all be a matter of luck, and occasionally giving luck a helping hand. Yes, that was it.

One thing, though, was plain. Tonight there was no lack of young and handsome men, many of whom were giving young girls like Emma bold and assessing looks—doubtless wondering how large their dowry was and whether they were worth pursuing. Thinking about dowries made her more than ever conscious that not only did she not possess one, but she also had the disadvantage of ignoble birth to overcome—if anyone ever found that out that she was illegitimate, that was.

To drive away these dreary thoughts she peered around the room from beneath her disfiguring cap, trying to discover if there was anyone present whom she might find worth pursuing.

There were a large number of men of all ages in uniform—was that where she ought to look for a possible husband, or should she try for one of the many beaux present? Perhaps an old beau might be more of an opportunity for her than a young one? The very thought made her shudder.

Emma looked over her shoulder at her and said plaintively, 'I wish that you were sitting beside me, Athene. I should not feel quite so sick.'

'Nonsense,' said Mrs Tenison robustly. 'You ought to be on your highest ropes at being here at all. Besides, I think that you may already have been found a partner. Cousin Exford expressly told me that he would introduce us to some suitable young men and here he comes with two splendid-looking fellows.'

Emma gave a small moan at this news. Athene, however, turned her grey eyes on the approaching Marquis of Exford and his companions to discover whether Mrs Tenison's description of them was at all apt.

Well, one of them, at least, was splendid. He was quite the most beautiful and well-dressed specimen of manhood she had ever seen, being blond, tall and of excellent address. The young man with him, however, could scarcely be described as splendid-looking in any way: formidable was a better word. He was tall, but he was built like a bruiser—as Athene had already learned boxers were called. He was as dark as his friend was fair, his face was strong and harsh, rather than Adonis-like, and his hair and eyes were as black as night.

Indeed, Athene found herself murmuring, 'Night and day.'

Mr Tenison overheard her and, turning his head a little in her direction, remarked in a voice equally low, 'Acute as ever, my dear—but which is which?'

This cryptic remark would have set Athene thinking if the Marquis had not already begun his introductions when the Tenison party stood up. Athene, already standing, wondered what piece of etiquette was demanded from her which would acknowledge the superior social standing of the Marquis and his guests. A small bob of the head might suffice, so she duly, and immediately, bobbed.

The slow dance of formalities began. It appeared that the fair young man was Adrian Drummond, Lord Kinloch, from Argyll, and that his companion was Mr Nicholas Cameron of Strathdene Castle in Sutherland. Emma blushed and stammered at them. The lowly companion was introduced as an afterthought. Nick and Adrian had spent the early part of the evening discreetly inspecting those young women present whom they had not seen before. As usual they had found little to please them. Nick indeed had gone so far as to mutter to Adrian, 'I don't think much of the current crop of beauties if this is the cream of it.'

Adrian had replied dolefully, 'Lord, yes. Mother is

going to be disappointed again. Not one of them is a patch on Kitty.'

His cousin could not but agree with him, and when their mutual relative, the Marquis of Exford, had come up to them saying enthusiastically, 'There's a pretty little filly here tonight that I think you two rogues ought to meet. That is, if you're both determined to marry, which Kinloch here says that you are,' Nick had groaned, 'Let him speak for himself— I'm in no great hurry to acquire a leg-shackle.'

Exford smiled mockingly. 'They're taking bets in the clubs that both of you will be hooked by the Season's end. If you really meant what you said, Cameron, I'll lay a few pounds on you *not* being reeled in. Let me know if you change your mind.'

Nick was not sure that he cared for being the subject of gossip and bets made by bored and light-minded men. Adrian, however, had smirked a little, much as he was now doing at Emma.

'Charmed to make your acquaintance,' he was saying, and he was not being completely untruthful. She was after all one of the best of the poor crop which he had so far encountered, being blonde and pretty if a touch pale. He thought that if he married her, providing himself with an heir was not going to be too difficult a task. Exford had also told him on the way over that she had a useful, if not a grand, portion.

Not of course, that that mattered overmuch. Owning half of Scotland—only the Duke of Sutherland was richer than Adrian—meant that he was able to indulge his fancy where a bride was concerned.

Athene realised from Emma's flutterings that she was finding this gorgeous specimen overwhelming: he was so different from the callow young men whom she had met at Assembly dances at home. When he bent down from his great height and said softly, 'I am already claimed for the first few dances, Miss Tenison, but I should be enchanted if you would stand up with me in the quadrille,' she went an unlovely scarlet, looked frantically first at Athene and then at her beaming mama, before saying, 'You do me too great an honour, Lord Kinloch.'

'Not at all,' he swiftly, and gallantly, replied. 'It is you who are doing me the honour, Miss Tenison.'

At this, Emma blushed again and agreed to stand up with him. Satisfied, Adrian said, still gallant, 'You will forgive me, I trust, if I leave you now. I must find my partner for the next dance. I shall be sure to visit you in good time for ours.'

Nick said to him when they strolled away to find their partners, 'I thought that she was going to faint when you asked her to dance. Are you sure that you wish to pursue such a shy creep-mouse? I will allow that she is pretty enough for you, but she would not be my choice for a wife.'

'Oh, I like 'em shy,' said his cousin, 'while you, you dog, like them talkative and striking—or in need of assistance in some way. I half-thought that you might have offered the companion a turn on the floor—it must be a great bore to stand up all night watching out for her charge.'

'You mean grey-eyed Pallas,' said Nick. 'One can only just detect the colour of Miss Filmer's eyes under that horrendous cap. She has a good figure, though, and by the cut of it she is not much older than her charge. Odd, that.'

'Pallas?' queried Adrian, puzzled. 'I thought that Emma's father said that her name was Athene.'

Nick laughed. It was patent that if Adrian had learned anything about the mythology of the ancient Greeks while he was at Oxford he had promptly forgotten it. 'Athene was the goddess of wisdom in the ancient world,' he said, 'and one of her names was grey-eyed Pallas. She had an owl as an attendant, too. I wonder if Miss Filmer sports one.'

'Should think not,' complained Adrian, 'not much use at a ball, owls. Nor at the theatre, either,' he added as an afterthought. 'You do come out with some weird things, Nick.'

Behind them Mrs Tenison was busily reproaching Emma for being so backward in welcoming Lord Kinloch's advances.

'I wonder at you, child, I really do. A handsome young man of great fortune makes a fuss of you and all that you can do is blush and stutter. Here is your great chance. Be sure to talk to him if he chooses to talk to you, and if he wishes to meet you again then by all means accept any invitation he cares to make.'

'But I really do feel sick, Mama,' faltered Emma. 'It is very hot in here—and he is so…so…'

She wanted to say that Adrian frightened her because he was like a prince in a fairy tale and surely he could not be interested in a country girl like herself.

Athene, listening to this, wondered why Mr Tenison did not defend his daughter a little. She thought wryly that if Lord Kinloch had asked her to dance with him she would have accepted his offer with alacrity—charming alacrity of course. While she felt sorry for Emma, she could not help feeling impatient with her. Now had the dark man, Nicholas Cameron, offered to stand up with her she could have understood her charge's reluctance.

She had not liked the assessing way in which he had looked at them. He had even examined her carefully—not that he could tell what she really looked like beneath her appalling turn-out. Was it possible that this whole business was a great mistake? How in the world was she ever going to be able to charm anyone while standing like an ill-dressed scarecrow, mute behind her unkind patroness?

Emma said again, 'I really do not feel very well, Mama,' to which her mother replied angrily, 'Stuff, Miss Tenison, stuff!'

Mr Tenison put in a gentle oar. 'Do you not think that you ought to take note of what our daughter is telling you, my dear?'

His wife turned on him angrily. 'No, indeed, Mr

Tenison. You ought to be aware of her whim-whams by now. It is time that she grew up. I do not hear Athene whining and wailing about her situation. If we give way to Emma every time she whimpers we might as well not have visited London at all.'

Mr Tenison subsided, and no wonder, thought Athene. He said not another word until Lord Kinloch returned with Nick in tow. He had cajoled him into offering the companion a turn on the floor. 'I need to get to know the family better,' being the bait he had offered his cousin. 'It would be as well to have the young dragon on my side.'

Nick had refrained from pointing out that judging by the dominant mother's behaviour the whole family would be on his side if he began to court Emma so that there was no need to humour the companion. But for all his good looks and self-assurance Adrian was basically modest.

In any case the poet Burns had once written that 'the best laid plans of mice and men gang aft agley'. Those of Adrian and Mrs Tenison certainly did. Adrian had scarcely had time to bow a welcome to Emma before she sprang to her feet, and face grey, fled from the ballroom, her hands over her mouth, wailing gently.

Mrs Tenison sprang to her feet also and charged after her. Athene was about to follow, but Mr Tenison now also standing exclaimed, 'No!' with unusual firmness and held her back. 'Her mother must care for her since it was she who has ignored her pleas for help.'

Adrian was completely nonplussed by this sudden turn of events which left him stranded on the edge of the ballroom floor, the centre of curious eyes. Nick had not yet had the opportunity to ask Miss Filmer to join him in the dance, nor was he to be allowed to do so.

With great address Mr Tenison sought to smooth over the unhappy situation created by Lord Kinloch's sudden loss of his partner, by saying, 'I am sure, Lord Kinloch, that you would wish to make up your set in the dance by taking Miss Filmer for your partner instead of Miss Emma. I am sure that my wife—and Emma—would prefer you not to be discommoded.'

To his great credit Adrian said, 'But, sir, what of your daughter? I should not like to entertain myself while she is ailing.'

'She rarely suffers these turns, but when she does they soon pass,' he said dryly. 'Athene, you would consent to partner Lord Kinloch, would you not?'

Would she not! Much though she regretted Emma's sudden collapse, Athene could not help but be delighted by this opportunity to get to know a rich and handsome young peer, a true Lord of All. Adrian hesitated a moment before offering her his hand, and saying, 'I would be grateful if you would oblige me, Miss Filmer.'

Her answer was to curtsey to him, bowing her head

a little when she did so—at which juncture her over-large cap fell forward on to the floor at Adrian's feet.

Deeply embarrassed, she had retrieved it and was about to resume it when Mr Tenison took it gently from her hand.

'Come, come, my dear, you do not need to take that disfiguring object with you into the dance for it to trouble Lord Kinloch with its misbehaviour. Is not that so, sir?'

Adrian did not hear him. He was too busy staring at the vision of beauty which was Athene Filmer now that she had lost her cap. She had, after entering the ballroom, visited one of the cloakrooms on a pretext and had loosened her hair from its painful and disfiguring bonds—which was why the cap had fitted so badly that it had come adrift. Even the horrid grey dress could not dim her loveliness. She reminded Adrian of the beautiful female statues he had seen on the Grand Tour which he had taken with Nick.

Nick was also staring at her. Grey-eyed Pallas, indeed, the very goddess herself. No owl, of course, but a pair of stern and dominant eyes which she was turning on the moonstruck Adrian above a subtle smile.

Now, what did that smile mean? Nick was a connoisseur of the human face. When he was in Italy he had come across an old folio containing drawings which purported to show that facial expressions almost invariably revealed the true thoughts and motives of those who assumed them. Experience had taught him that these very often slight indicators usually told him something important about those who displayed them.

He didn't gamble very often—he considered it a fool's pastime—but his ability to read the faces of those against whom he played gave him a marked advantage over them whenever he chose to. In the case of the one beautiful young woman whom he had hoped to make his wife he had ignored some reveal-ing signs, only to discover later that they had told him correctly of her lack of virtue—thus adding to his suspicion of women's motives.

So, what was the true meaning of Miss Athene Filmer's smile? It was not at all the smile of a woman dumb-struck by Adrian's physical beauty. Miss Emma Tenison—and many other women—had worn that smile, but not this particular woman. Unless he were mistaken, it resembled nothing less than that of someone who has achieved something important: it was the smile of a man who was winning a game of tennis, or that of an angler who was about to land a large fish.

Oh, she was a dangerous creature, was she not? A true beauty with her dark hair, her grey eyes and her glorious figure… And what the devil was he doing, standing there, drooling over such a fair deceiver, even if she were named after the goddess of wisdom herself?

He shook himself to restore his usual cold self-possession and began to pay attention to Mr Tenison, who was asking him to sit by him for a while since both of them were now abandoned while Adrian cavorted with Pallas Athene on the dance floor. Nick was only too ready to oblige him. He wanted to know more about this unlikely beauty. At first he and Mr Tenison spoke of general matters: the Season, the news from Spain, the wretched business of Luddism in the Midland counties.

It seemed that his family, and their companion, lived not far from Steepwood Abbey, where, if Nick were not mistaken, there had recently been yet another major scandal concerning its owner, the debauched Marquis of Sywell. He had taken some nobody for a wife—presumably no one else would have him—and the nobody had suddenly, and mysteriously, disappeared. It had even been suggested that Sywell had done away with her, which, considering his reputation, was a not unreasonable assumption.

Since nothing further had occurred, either in the lady's reappearing, or Sywell or someone else being accused of disposing of her, the scandal had finally died down, and would only be revived if there were any further, exciting revelations.

'Are you acquainted with Sywell, sir?' Nick asked. 'Is he such a monster as rumour says he is?'

'Worse,' said Mr Tenison briefly. 'No, I am not acquainted with him—who is? I am at present, however, disputing some boundary lines with him. He has seen fit to enclose a large portion of my lands, not that he intends to do anything useful with it, of course, just to be a thorough nuisance to yet another of his neighbours.'

Nick nodded; so Sywell was the miserable scoundrel which the *on dit* said he was, and a bad neighbour into the bargain. He thought that now was the time for him to find out a little about Pallas Athene. So, while he was apparently idly watching her busily charming his cousin whenever they were joined in the dance, he said, 'Your daughter's companion seems strangely young for her post. They are usually middle-aged, or elderly, dragons. This one seems scarcely older than her charge.'

'Oh, yes,' said Mr Tenison, responding to this apparently reasonable statement. 'As you have seen, my dear little Emma is of a nervous disposition. My wife thought that the usual stern creature we might hire would overwhelm her. Fortunately she was able to find someone sensible who would guard her and whom Emma would not be afraid of but would obey. Miss Filmer was a few years ahead of Emma at her school and protected her from those who sought to bully her because of her timidity. It also meant that she was doing Miss Filmer a kindness by giving her the opportunity to come to London for the Season, something her widowed mother could not otherwise afford.'

If Mr Tenison was crediting his wife with a benevolence which she did not possess, Nick was not to know that. He had, however, learned something useful. The poor girl from the provinces had been handed an unlooked-for opportunity to make the acquaintance of one of the United Kingdom's richest young men. Hence, of course, the smile.

He might be doing her a wrong but he thought not. His instincts, finely honed over the years, told him that he was correct, particularly when Mr Tenison added innocently, 'Miss Filmer is a most unusual girl, since she is not only beautiful, but remarkably clever, something which my dear Emma is not. We have had some interesting conversations in which she has shown an intellectual maturity far beyond her years. I consider that we are fortunate to have her as Emma's companion—something of that must surely rub off on her.'

Nick, from the little he had seen of Miss Emma Tenison, sincerely doubted that! Mr Tenison's revelations told him that Athene was well-named, but only time would reveal whether or not he was judging her too harshly in believing her to be husband-hunting for herself.

On the dance floor Athene was busy doing exactly what he thought that she was about.

At first she was pleasantly demure, but when Adrian said in his cheerful way, 'I do hope that you are allowed to enjoy yourself a little, Miss Filmer. Standing around keeping an eye on that timid little thing must be dull work.'

'Oh, Mr Tenison has been extremely kind to me,' she ventured prettily. 'Did he not ensure that I have not lacked for a partner tonight by recommending me to you? I trust that by doing so when Emma had her *crise de nerfs* just now he has not discommoded you.'

Adrian, who was not at all sure that he knew what a *crise de nerfs* was, and hoped that it was not catching, said artlessly, 'Dear Miss Filmer, I was absolutely charmed by my first sight of you when you lost your ugly cap, and was delighted tò have you for a partner instead of the mouse.'

Suddenly aware that in being so gallant to Athene he had impolitely slighted her charge, he added hastily, 'Not that I meant anything wrong about Miss Emma, not at all…' He rapidly ran down, aware that anything he said might make matters worse.

'Oh, quite,' said Athene. 'Poor little thing, it is quite an affliction with her. Crowds always seem to depress her.'

'But not you, I'll be bound,' offered Adrian. The dance temporarily parting them, he spent the next few moments thinking up compliments which would not offend and congratulating himself on having found a real beauty. No chance of not being able to provide Clan Drummond with the wanted heir if he married, and bedded, her!

By the time the dance ended Athene had managed to convey that if Lord Kinloch was charmed by her, she was charmed by him. She had given him the address of the Tenisons' town house after he had informed her that he wished to further their acquaintance. He was not so stupid as to be unaware that the only way in which he could see more of Athene was by showing an interest in the mouse.

Or perhaps he could persuade Nick to appear to pursue the mouse whilst he cultivated Athene. On second thoughts that was not a good idea. Nick would never agree to deceive a woman by pretending to admire her. He was too stupidly honest for that.

Nick, meanwhile, was further cultivating Mr Tenison by discussing with him Plato and his notions about morality, until Mrs Tenison returned, a somewhat recovered Emma in tow.

'A drink of water with a little brandy in it has restored the dear child,' she announced, before looking around her to discover that Athene and Lord Kinloch were both missing.

'Where in the world has Filmer disappeared to, Mr Tenison? I trust that she is not ailing, too. That would be the outside of enough. Emma needs her protection.'

Mr Tenison allowed apologetically that he had suggested that Lord Kinloch having lost his partner, he might still enjoy his dance if Miss Filmer acted as a substitute for Emma.

'Indeed,' said Mrs Tenison frostily. She looked at Nick and decided that he would not do as a partner for Emma. He was not a lord, and she had never heard of him. He was not on the list of eligible young men which she and her sponsor, Lady Dunlop, had drawn up between them.

Nick was saved by the return of Adrian and Pallas

Athene from asking Emma, to whom he had offered his chair, to be his partner in the next dance. Athene, delighted that Lord Kinloch was so obviously taken by her, adopted a suitably demure manner when he gallantly insisted on handing her to a chair instead of restoring her to her usual humble station behind the Tenisons. She had no wish to offend Mrs Tenison more than was necessary. If she were to do so she might find herself sent back to Northampton.

That lady took one look at her radiant face—so different from Emma's pale one—and barked at her, 'Where is your cap, Filmer? What have you done with it?'

To Athene's amusement, Adrian, wounded a little on his beauty's behalf, said tactlessly, 'It fell off, madam, because it did not fit Miss Filmer properly, and she is not a dull old thing who needs to wear something to hide her lack of looks!'

If this reproach both pleased and amused Athene, it stung Mrs Tenison, who now had the task of placating the young man whom she had mentally marked down as a prospect for Emma.

'Oh, quite,' she said, while looking to her husband for guidance, something which she rarely did. 'Most proper of you, Lord Kinloch. You may leave it off in future, Miss Filmer.'

Oh, so she was Miss Filmer now, was she? And Lord Kinloch had just saved her from the humiliation of wearing her dreadful cap. She had barely time to take in these two momentous concessions when she registered that Mr Cameron was looking at her with the oddest expression on his face. If Nick was experienced in the art of reading other people's expressions well, Athene, who was a novice just acquiring this necessary skill, was already acute enough to grasp that, for some reason, Mr Nicholas Cameron did not approve of her.

Well, pooh, to that, he was not the man in whom she was interested, although judging by the manner in which the cousins spoke to one another it would be as well not to antagonise him.

She had scarcely had time to think this before she was astonished to find Nick bowing to her, and saying in his deep, gravel voice, quite unlike Lord Kinloch's charming, light tenor, 'I trust that you will do me the honour of standing up with me in the next dance, Miss Filmer.'

Here was another splendid opportunity to cement her new-found friendship with Lord Kinloch and all his hangers-on.

'I should be delighted, sir,' she replied, casting her eyes innocently down.

If she was not fooling herself in her pursuit of Adrian, neither was she fooling Nick. He could scarcely suppress a grin when he put out his hand to take her on to the floor.

'Athene,' he said to her charming profile. 'Grey-eyed Pallas. May one ask if you own an owl as well?'

He wondered if she were educated enough to catch the allusion. Athene turned towards him, and if grey eyes could ever glitter, hers glittered. Conversation with Mr Cameron was obviously going to be of quite a different order from that with his cousin. She wondered what Mr Tenison had been saying to him.

She decided to be honest and not pretend charming innocence. 'I only possess the name of the Greek goddess of wisdom, Mr Cameron, not her attributes. Owls are in short supply in our part of Northampton.'

'But not wisdom, I suppose. Tell me, does your young charge frequently suffer from these fits?'

There was something slightly cutting in his tone. They had reached their set, so she turned to face him before the dance began.

'They are not fits, Mr Cameron,' she told him coolly, 'and I am sure that when you and Mr Tenison conversed he spoke to you of them. I am merely her companion, not her physician, but they are, I am sure, nervous only and when she becomes more confident will pass in time.'

'And do *you* intend to help her to be more confident, Miss Filmer? I would have thought that the presence of another young woman as much in command of herself as you seem to be might have the effect of distressing, rather than helping, her.'

'Then you thought wrongly again,' she told him, sure now by his tone of voice and his expression that he was her enemy, although why she could not imagine. 'I happen to be able to comfort Miss Tenison. I have done so since we were at school together. It is others who have the opposite effect on her.'

She did not say, most of all her dominant mother, for that would have been neither proper nor polite. She was surprised that Mr Nicholas Cameron, who seemed a perceptive young man, had not noticed how much Emma's mama extinguished her.

'We are,' she went on, 'likely to make a spectacle of ourselves if we do not end our conversation immediately and ready ourselves for the dance as everyone else in our set has done.'

Oh, bravo, Miss Filmer, was Nick's internal reaction to this. You are all and more what I thought you were: a resourceful adventuress on the make. One thing is also certain: cousin Adrian will be no match for such a determined creature as you are proving to be.

Later he was to ask himself why he felt such hostility to the mere idea that Athene Filmer would trap his cousin into marriage, but at the time he was not yet able to consider her, or her apparent wiles, dispassionately.

The dance passed without further conversation, leaving Nick to discover that Miss Filmer's body, beneath her disfiguring grey gown, was as he had already supposed, as classically lovely as her face. He could not be surprised when, on the way home, his cousin Adrian spent the whole journey talking enthusiastically of Miss Filmer's beauty and charm.

'A stunner,' he kept exclaiming. 'A very stunner—don't you agree, Nick?'

Yes, Nick did agree, but although he also distrusted

Athene's motives in pursuing his cousin, he didn't think that it was yet politic to be critical of her. Like many not over-bright young men, Adrian could be extraordinarily obstinate, and Nick knew from experience that to oppose him at this point would make him even more determined to admire this new beauty to grace the London scene.

All he said was, mildly, 'I wonder who her people are? Listening to Mrs Tenison I gained the impression that she would not have approved of a total nobody being her daughter's friend and companion.'

Adrian snorted. 'She's a poor little creep-mouse, the daughter, isn't she? Not a bit like my Athene.'

My Athene! Goodness, thought Nick, amused, one dance and an hour of her company and he's really taken the bait to the degree that he thinks of her as his.

'I can't remember you having been so besotted with a female before on such a short acquaintance,' he ventured. 'We really know nothing of her.'

'Only that she's in good society, is beautiful and says jolly things,' riposted Adrian. 'I noticed that you were chattering away with her before the dance started. What in the world did you find to talk about if you weren't impressed by her looks and address?'

'Owls,' said Nick gravely. 'Owls. Apparently they are rather scarce in the wilds of Northampton.'

'Owls!' exclaimed Adrian. 'That's not what pretty girls like to talk about. If that's all you could think of to interest her, it's no wonder she didn't impress, or charm you.'

Nick refrained from telling him that he didn't think that Miss Athene Filmer was trying very hard to charm him, and that he, far from charming Miss Filmer himself, had been rather short with her.

Yes, the less said the better. Perhaps Adrian would grow bored with having to keep up mentally with the clever creature which he judged Miss Filmer to be. He would be far better off with the creep-mouse who would make no intellectual demands on him and who had spent the rest of the evening staring adoringly at him, but was unhappily aware that Lord Kinloch only had eyes and ears for her beautiful companion.

In the meantime he would keep careful watch over them both, for he felt certain that the besotted Adrian would be chasing as hard as he could the beauty who he hoped would rescue him from his mother's reproaches by consenting to marry him and thus give Kinloch lands an heir.

CHAPTER TWO

'If you are to accompany us to Madame Félice's, Filmer, then you must wear your cap, but you may leave it off when you go into society since it seems to distress Lord Kinloch.'

Of all things Mrs Tenison wished to please Lord Kinloch. He was quite the grandest young man who had been presented to Emma since she had arrived in London, and Mrs Tenison took his wish to be allowed to call on them as soon as possible to mean that he was showing an interest in her daughter.

Lady Dunlop had told Mrs Tenison that if she wished Emma to cut a dash in London society then she must be dressed by the fashionable *modiste*, Madame Félice. Mrs Tenison had seen at once that Emma's clothes, whilst considered charming in the provinces, were by no means fit for a young woman who wished to be admired when she was presented to the Prince Regent.

Madame Félice's shop was in Bond Street, that

Mecca of the rich and the pretentious. The lady herself was famous not only for her taste, but for her beauty. She had arrived from nowhere: the *on dit* was that she must have a rich protector, because only that could explain how she had managed to find the money, not only to buy such prestigious premises, but also to furnish them in the best possible taste.

Athene was walking sedately behind Emma, her mama, and Lady Dunlop, who was again acting as their patron in this matter, for Madame Félice, it appeared, did not make clothes for everyone, but chose her customers carefully. She could only look around her and marvel since, except for a few long mirrors, strategically placed, they might have been in one of the drawing-rooms of the ton. A pretty young woman showed them to a long sofa before which was an occasional table graced by a bowl of spring flowers. There was no sign of either Madame Félice or the clothes which she designed and sold. Their escort offered them lemonade from a silver pitcher before departing to notify her of their arrival.

'The workrooms are at the back,' said Lady Dunlop reverently. She was another large woman, like Mrs Tenison and possessed, if possible, even more address. She was the widow of a one-time Lord Mayor of London and was consequently immensely rich. 'You will understand that French is Madame's first language but she speaks tolerable English. Ah, here she comes.'

Madame was as elegant as one might have expected. Her day gown was pale blue in colour, high-waisted and classically cut. Its small ruffled linen collar was tied with a simple bow. Emma, who had been a little worried that she might be expected to wear something *outré,* was relieved to see that Madame's toilette was of the plainest. Indeed, she would have worn it with pleasure herself. For her part, Athene could only wish that Madame was going to design clothes for her.

It was only when she drew near, greeting them all with a bow when they rose to meet her, that Athene had the oddest sensation that she had met Madame before. This was of course, a nonsense, since Lady Dunlop had told them that Madame had come from Paris via the Low Countries some time during the last two years, but had only recently set up in Bond Street.

'Pray be seated,' she told them in prettily accented English, before seating herself in a high-backed chair after Lady Dunlop had carried out the necessary introductions. 'I understand that it is Miss Tenison I am to dress. It will be both a challenge and a pleasure, since I must retain her charming innocence and yet create something which will be sure to attract attention. A difficult feat, that, but I am sure that it can be managed.'

Her eyes roved over Athene when she added, 'I am not required to dress Miss Filmer also?'

Mrs Tenison, having beamed at Madame's description of Emma, now bridled a little at the mention of Athene.

'By no means. I fear that Miss Filmer cannot afford the fees you will be charging.'

'A pity,' said Madame sweetly. 'No matter, we will concentrate on Miss Tenison's requirements.'

She proceeded to do so. A bevy of young women were summoned and came in carrying pattern books, bolts of silk, satin and gauze, lengths of ribbon and made-up silk posies of a kind which she said that she would create for Emma. A small sketchbook and pencil was handed to Madame, who began to draw very rapidly a series of elegant garments for Emma. She showed the sketches to Emma and asked her opinion of the style and the colours which she had chosen.

Mrs Tenison, always dominant, objected to this as firmly as politeness would allow, saying, 'I would prefer, if you please, to select my daughter's coming-out gowns myself. I am not sure that she is necessarily the best judge of what will suit her.'

Emma, who had been enjoying herself immensely, and had once or twice called on Athene to help her, hung her head a little at this and looked frantically first at Madame and then at Athene, who was the amused spectator of Madame's manipulations and who had also just remembered where she had seen the *modiste* before.

From the moment that Madame had begun to draw, Athene had recognised her. She knew at once where it was that she had last seen that intent and highly concentrated expression and who had worn it.

Yet, could it be possible? Could it be that Madame

Félice, so fine, so polished, who had recently arrived in London from Paris via the Low Countries, was in reality harum-scarum, flyaway, country-bred, ill-dressed Louise Hanslope with whom she had played as a child? Louise, the daughter of a mysterious never-seen French émigré, who had been adopted by the Hanslopes in place of the child it seemed that they could never have.

Later she had been sent away to Northampton to be apprenticed to a dressmaker, and she and Athene had corresponded with one another even though Louise was some years older than she was.

Now she knew that the lonely child which Louise had been had taken delight in befriending another lonely and unhappy little girl. Later when she had returned to become the Marchioness of Sywell their friendship had been renewed and the two of them had roamed the Abbey grounds enjoying its neglected, but wildly beautiful, scenery.

The last time she had seen Louise before she disappeared had been at the old Rune Stone, set in a stand of trees which was always known as the Sacred Grove. They had been painting it from different angles and she had looked up to see that Louise was lost in the world which she was creating on paper. Athene's own efforts, although creditable, showed nothing of the great talent for colour and design which Louise's possessed and which she was now turning to good account in her profitable business.

Perhaps she was mistaken. Athene thought not. She

was sure that she, and she alone, had discovered that the missing Marchioness was not dead, not starving in a garret, but was a rich and successful *modiste* serving the wives of the great ones of the world of society!

And now little Louise Hanslope was saying smoothly to Mrs Tenison, 'You may offer me your opinion, madame, but I must remind you that it is Miss Emma who will wear my clothes and she will not be happy in them if they are not to her taste.'

'But they are so extremely simple,' protested Mrs Tenison.

'It is charming innocence that I am dressing, re-member?' countered Madame Félice. 'If you are not happy with what I am proposing then I suggest that you go elsewhere,' and she began to close her draw-ing-book.

Lady Dunlop shook her elegantly coiffed head at Mrs Tenison, who said hastily, 'Oh, no, madame, I am in your hands. Do as you think fit.'

Athene could scarce repress a laugh at this abject surrender by the tyrant. She gave a little cough, while Emma, released for the first time from the bondage of her dominant mama, said eagerly, 'Oh, Madame Félice, I have the most splendid notion. Would it be possible for all my gowns, however they are cut and in whatever material, to be white in colour? I think that it would suit me, particularly if you make me some sprays of lily-of-the-valley, white crocuses and small freesias to wear with them. I have always wanted to wear white.'

It was the first occasion on which Emma had ever asserted herself, and Athene could not fault her taste, so far removed from the dull and often garish toilettes which had been her mother's choice.

'But...' began Mrs Tenison, only to meet Madame's stern eye, and mutter, 'Oh, very well.'

After that, all went swimmingly. Madame and Emma, between them, finished with a splendidly simple wardrobe. Athene, still amused, managed to catch Madame's eye when she was inspecting a length of white silk which one of her minions was holding against Emma. Since she was out of Mrs Tenison and Lady Dunlop's line of sight she indulged herself in a daring wink, which had been one of her and Louise's jokes in the old days. Madame did not wink, but gave her a slow and meaningful smile.

Oh, yes, she had not been wrong! She had found her old friend, strangely changed. Now all that was left was to renew their friendship, although how she was to do so in front of the two harpies, as Athene naughtily thought of them, might be difficult.

She had not allowed for Madame Félice's resourcefulness. Before their session was over, that lady, on some pretext, retired to the workrooms at the back of the shop, returning a little later with some small sprays of white silk flowers, already made up as specimens of what she could do, and a pile of paper. After a short interval she handed Athene the paper to hold, having first made sure that none of her minions was near her.

'You will oblige me, I am sure,' she said to the poor companion who had stood, unheeded, throughout the lengthy morning. 'They are some sketches I have made which might it amuse you to look through while we conclude our business.'

Her French accent was stronger than ever when she came out with this. Athene duly obliged her by taking the papers and looking through them.

The first one was, as Madame had said, a drawing of a walking dress which would have suited Athene down to the ground, as the saying had it. Beneath it Madame had written, 'You would look well in this.'

The second paper had no sketch drawn on it. Instead a short note in Madame's fine hand said, 'I see that my old friend is not deceived. Is it possible that our friendship could be renewed? Surely the slave has some time of her own and could visit one who is a slave no longer?'

The note was unsigned, but its message was plain. Madame Félice, or rather, Louise, the Marchioness of Sywell, wished to meet her, away from her charge and the harpies.

Unobserved, Athene spent the remainder of the visit looking through the rest of the papers, which were all drawings of the most elegant gowns, coats, bonnets, gloves, and even parasols. Occasionally, she showed one to Lady Dunlop to admire. Mrs Tenison was too busy agonisedly watching Emma being fitted out in what she privately considered to be the most unsuitable clothing to be able to take note of anything else.

Eventually everyone but Mrs Tenison was satisfied and prepared to leave. Athene handed the papers back to Madame Félice, saying, 'My thanks, Madame. They were most instructive and I shall be sure to follow your advice.'

Madame smiled sweetly and said, 'I am delighted that I was able to offer you assistance. It has been a pleasure to dress Miss Emma—I think that she is someone who will improve when her confidence grows. I trust, Miss Filmer, that you will be of equal assistance to her.'

Athene nodded, guiltily realising that in her efforts to attract Lord Kinloch, far from helping Emma, she was taking his attention away from her! On the other hand, there would be many young men who would be only too happy to court Emma—or 'make a leg at her,' as the current fashionable slang had it, so she was not really depriving her of anything serious.

Nevertheless, what her old friend had said had made her feel uncomfortable, and she tried to console herself with the thought that if she did not look after herself, no one else would.

She took that thought with her into the drawing-room that afternoon when Lord Kinloch—with his attendant cousin—paid his promised visit to them. She had already decided that during her one afternoon off she would visit Bond Street and renew her friendship with Louise—or rather Madame Félice as she must now think of her.

She wondered crossly whether Lord Kinloch ever went anywhere without his interfering shadow: she was unhappily aware of Nick's sardonic eye on her, even though she sat, all prim and proper, a little away from the main company. She was not wearing her cap, for after some strong—and private—words between Mrs Tenison and her husband, she had been informed after nuncheon that she was to leave it off in future.

Adrian was on his high ropes at the prospect of seeing Athene again, although for form's sake he had to address most of his conversation to the Tenisons.

'I have the most interesting news for you,' he announced jovially. 'I have decided that now that I have acquired a curricle I shall waste no time in racing it to Brighton. I intend to make it known that I am ready to accept any wager from anyone.'

'A reasonable wager, I trust,' said Nick sardonically.

'Of course,' said Adrian grandly—although no such proviso had entered his head. 'I am not so green as to waste my fortune on it.'

Nick refrained from pointing out that his cousin had had little or no practice in driving his new toy, and to race it before he was fully ready to do so might be unwise, if not to say dangerous.

It was left to Mr Tenison to say reflectively, 'I believe that curricle racing is not without danger, Lord

Kinloch. Only the other week two reckless young men were racing at full speed towards Brighton and found themselves side by side on the road in the way of a large cart being driven by a farm labourer. All three vehicles ended up in the ditch. One of the young men broke his arm and the other his leg.'

Athene could not resist asking, 'What happened to the poor labourer?'

'History does not relate,' said Nick. 'It dealt only with two feckless idiots, and had little to say on the matter of the one poor soul trying to earn a living and who had been deprived of the ability to do so.'

'I think,' said Adrian, 'that you may safely rely on me not to do anything foolish.'

Nick, knowing Adrian's cheerful, if not to say feckless, optimism, doubted that very much. But he did not wish to give his cousin a put-down before the Tenisons.

Emma, however, remarked anxiously, 'It sounds very dangerous to me. I beg of you to take care, Lord Kinloch, if you engage in anything so adventurous.'

'It's little more so than riding a horse,' declaimed Adrian, who had already had this argument with Nick and was determined not to be put off something which was so dear to his heart. 'Lots of fellows have raced to Brighton without coming to grief.'

Athene privately thought that Adrian was hardly the man to succeed in a venture which needed both skill and judgement beyond the common run, but she decided to say nothing, until Nick came out somewhat provocatively with, 'And you, Miss Filmer, what do you think of Lord Kinloch's engaging in this tricky pastime?'

'That it is not for me to question his judgement in the matter, since I have not yet seen him driving his curricle. If and when he feels that he is ready to take on all comers, then we must respect his decision.'

Nick could not help thinking, his expression growing more sardonic than ever, that Miss Filmer ought to be a man and then her talent for tactful and double-dealing answers could be put to practical use. His respect for her intellect grew as rapidly as his dislike for her apparent duplicity!

'Bravo, Miss Filmer,' said Adrian, who was quite unaware of the nuances in Athene's answer. 'So happy to see that not all of my friends are killjoys. You will be sure to cheer me on when I do decide to race.'

'Indeed, Lord Kinloch.'

'Come, come,' he said, beaming around on them all, 'since you are now my friends I must be Adrian to the ladies and Kinloch to you, sir,' he ended, addressing Mr Tenison.

Such gracious condescension was meat and drink to Emma's mother. Unaware that Athene was M'lord's real target and not Emma, she drowned him in effusive thanks, already thinking of the happy day when she would be able to speak of Emma to her friends as 'My daughter, Lady Kinloch'. She had, however, already added Nick to her lengthy list of people whom she disliked.

Mr Tenison remarked dryly, 'Nevertheless, Kinloch, I am bound to support Mr Cameron's reservations about the wisdom of your trying to race after such a short period of practice.'

His wife said sharply, 'It is just like you, Mr Tenison, to throw cold water over young people's pleasures. I am sure that Lord Kinloch knows what he is doing. We shall certainly cheer you on whenever you do race you may be sure of that, m'lord!'

Conversation, which had been general, now became particular. Adrian addressed himself to the three women, while Mr Tenison quietly continued his conversation of the previous evening with Nick, which had been interrupted by Emma's return.

'If the others would not consider it impolite, I would like to invite you to take a short turn in my library. I have a rare edition there of Burton's Anatomy of Melancholy, of which we spoke last night and which you might like to inspect.'

Adrian, overhearing this, said benevolently, 'By all means, sir. Take Nick to the library. Grubbing among the books will restore his high spirits.'

Nick said slowly, 'If our hostess agrees…'

Mrs Tenison rapidly interrupted him. 'By all means, Mr Tenison. We must keep our guests happy.'

She was delighted to learn that she and Emma— and Filmer, of course, but she didn't count—were to be left alone with Adrian. She was even more delighted when Nick, the spirit of mischief moving in him, added, 'On one condition, sir: that Miss Filmer accompanies us. I gather from something you said last night that she is something of a bookworm, too.'

Now, what's *his* little game, thought Athene inelegantly, and furiously. Oh yes, I have it, he's moving me from Adrian's orbit so that he is compelled to concentrate on Emma, and not me.

There was no way, however, in which she could refuse such an offer, which was enthusiastically seconded by Mr Tenison who thought—wrongly—that it would be a great opportunity for Athene not to have to join in the vapid conversation which would surely follow when the only persons of sense were removed from the room.

Nick, a subtle smile on his face, held out his arm to what he knew was the reluctant Athene, who was compelled to present a smiling face to the world at being singled out for such an honour. He knew that on the way home Adrian would roast him mightily for removing Athene from a place where he could see and worship her from afar. After all, had she not virtually approved of his decision to race to Brighton when everyone else had been so dashed dispiriting over the matter?

Adrian would like to bet that if ladies were encouraged to race curricles Athene would be a splendid performer. The image of her urging her team on entranced him so much that he barely heard what the two Tenison women were saying to him. Or rather,

Mrs Tenison, for Emma merely sat there, silently worshipping his handsome presence much as he had been worshipping Athene's.

Athene, meanwhile, was listening to Nick and Mr Tenison talk about Burton, whose book she had not yet read although Mr Tenison had recommended it to her. He had fetched it from its shelf and laid it on the big map table which stood in front of the window for Nick to inspect it.

After a short—and enthusiastic—examination of it, while Athene stood by, Nick said, 'I fear that we may be boring Miss Filmer.'

Athene returned, a trifle sharply, 'Not at all. I find it most interesting to listen to Mr Tenison—he offers me an education which I would not otherwise have achieved.'

Mr Tenison smiled at this and murmured, 'You see, sir, she is truly named Athene, and like the great Pallas herself no one could call her a bluestocking.'

'No, indeed,' agreed Nick. 'Miss Filmer is neither plain nor noisy—a very model of rectitude.'

Athene could have hit him. She now knew him well enough to know that he was roasting her. Mr Tenison was taking Nick's words at face value, and nodding vigorous agreement.

He removed the copy of Burton, reached down to a low shelf on which stood a run of giant folios, and lifted out one which he laid reverently on the table before opening it and saying to the pair of them, 'I'm sure that you would find this splendid volume of great interest. It contains the most wonderful engravings of all the Greek gods, including Athene who is pictured here with her owl.'

That owl again! For the first time Nick and Athene exchanged a smile at its reappearance. The smile's effect on them both was electric. Nick's harsh face, which Athene had always thought of as sour, was strangely softened when the light of humour danced in his eyes. Its sternness disappeared, and his attraction grew as his smile widened. Athene's face, too, changed. The touch of hauteur, which was the consequence of her feeling that she needed to defend herself in the face of a cruel and critical world, disappeared from it.

Each recognised in the other a similar understanding of the true nature of that world, and each of them was disconcerted to discover that the other possessed it, too. To cover their confusion both of them put forward a hand at the same time to point out something which interested them in the portrayal of the goddess—and their hands met.

The effect of this simple touch, coming as it did on the heels of the smile, surprised them both, since neither of them had experienced anything similar when they had danced together at the Leominsters' ball. It was as though a fire ran through them. For a moment they were locked together in a universe where only the other existed.

Mr Tenison, unaware of their strange epiphany, or moment of understanding, continued to speak, taking his hearers' silence for an appreciation of what he was showing them. Athene was the first to recover from the odd bodily sensations which touching Nick had induced. She wrenched her hand away and began to rub it, wondering why in the world she had responded in this strange manner to someone whom she disliked and who plainly disliked her.

Nick was in no doubt as to what had happened. Good God! Of all wretched things! He had fallen in lust with the siren who was chasing after his cousin! He was self-knowing enough to ask whether that was why he resented her so much—that he was jealous because he was not the object of her pursuit. No matter. He sternly told his unruly body to behave itself, for once he had had this dreadful thought arousal had not been long to follow.

For a brief moment they had been together, but now they were apart again. Athene, as strongly aroused as Nick, but in her innocence unaware of what had happened to her, made what she thought of as distracted conversation although Mr Tenison appeared to notice nothing odd.

'Was Pallas Athene what we would call a witch?' she asked, unaware that Nick, now recovered, was sardonically thinking: the goddess might not have been a witch but you plainly are, to have such an effect on me.

Mr Tenison considered her question seriously. 'In our terms yes, but I do not think that the Greeks thought of her as one.'

He turned the pages and, silent, his hearers allowed him to continue his impromptu lecture until he pulled his watch from its pocket and exclaimed, 'Goodness. It is time that we returned. I have no wish to fail in politeness to your cousin, but I am of the opinion that the library would not interest him.'

'Not at all,' said Nick, and, lying in his teeth, he added, 'Besides, I am sure that Kinloch is only too delighted not to have to share your daughter's conversation with me.'

'She does not care for the library overmuch,' said Emma's father mournfully. 'On the other hand, Miss Filmer does, and as you have already heard she asks the most interesting questions.'

Nick had discovered more than that about Athene, but he could not tell Mr Tenison of it.

They returned to find Adrian holding forth about the coming race again. Before he and Nick left to show themselves in Hyde Park, to which he had promised to drive the Tenisons in the near future, his last words were, 'I am sure you will not regret coming to watch the start at Westminster Bridge when I do race. It will be the most tremendous fun.'

On her first afternoon off Athene made her way to Bond Street and Madame Félice's shop. She was burning to know how Louise Hanslope, who had become the Marchioness of Sywell, had managed to disappear and transform herself into society's most sought-after *modiste* when half Northamptonshire had been looking for her dead body.

She remembered Emma saying to her with a shiver, 'Oh, Athene, do you think that the Steepwood curse has struck again and is responsible for her disappearance, or, hateful thought, her death? After all, everyone in the district knows that those who live on what was once sacred ground do so under the threat of reaching a terrible end—and the Abbey is sacred ground.'

Athene had said as gently as she could, 'Oh, that's superstitious nonsense, my love, of the kind one reads about in Mrs Radcliffe's novels, all of which happen in foreign parts. The English countryside is not the place where murder and kidnappings occur.'

'But she *is* missing,' Emma had said mournfully.

There was no answer to that, and now, improbably, Athene was about to find out the truth. Fortunately neither Emma nor Mrs Tenison had known Louise when she had been the Marchioness, so they had not recognised her in her guise of Madame Félice.

Athene's old friend greeted her with pleasure and a loving kiss before leading her upstairs into her living quarters above the shop. There, in a pretty room overlooking the street, she rang for tea and biscuits to be brought for herself and her guest.

'Now,' she said, when the little maid had returned with the tea board, 'we may have a jolly coze together. You must be wondering how I arrived in Bond Street and I am all agog to know how you came to

be poor little Emma's companion. Poor, you understand, because I can see that she is under the thumb
of her dreadful mother. She is an object of pity despite
her splendid dowry.'

Athene again began to suffer pangs of conscience
when she thought of how hard she was scheming to
make Adrian Kinloch propose to her and not to
Emma.

She tried to dismiss them by saying, 'Oh, my story
is simple. Mrs Tenison had enough common-sense to
grasp that if she gave Emma another taskmistress as
hard as she is herself, the poor child would have been
extinguished. In the guise of being kind to Mama and
myself, she offered me bed and board for the Season
in return for acting as Emma's companion.'

'You mean that the old baggage is not paying you?'
gasped Louise incredulously. 'She is treating you
worse than she would a servant!'

'Indeed, but since I am by way of being a gentlewoman the pretence is that it would not be proper to
offer me a fee. Do not worry overmuch on my behalf,
though. Mr Tenison is kind and gives me free run of
the library and his conversation.'

'I trust that he is not too kind,' said Louise suspi-
ciously. 'Gentlemen of a certain age, particularly
when they have wives like Mrs T., are not to be
trusted near pretty young ladies of any age. And despite your appalling clothing you are a very pretty
young lady indeed.'

'Well, so far he has said and done nothing wrong,

and somehow, I don't think he will. But if he did, I would think up some excuse to return home immediately, you may be sure of that.'

'I'm happy to hear it. I always thought that you had a fund of downright common-sense. And now I suppose that I ought to tell you my story, which is a deal more like a novel by Mrs Radcliffe than is comfortable. There was a time when I thought such adventures as mine were simply the stuff of idle tales for idle ladies. No such luck for me, though. In an evil hour, mistaking the man completely, for remember, I was still young and green, I married the Marquis of Sywell. It was the worst day's work I ever embarked on. Before marriage he sought to charm me, after marriage, no such thing. I was his prisoner and his slave....'

She broke off and turned away from Athene, who reached out to put a gentle hand on her arm, saying, 'Do not continue, my dear, if it distresses you.'

'No,' said Louise, pulling herself together and regaining her normal composure. 'It is not only that to speak of it distresses me, but I cannot tell you, an innocent, unmarried female, of what that terrible man made me suffer... Suffice that suffer I did, and in ways of which I could not speak to anyone.

'One day at my wits' end, and terrified that he might kill me in one of his fits of cruel rage, I decided to run away and try to begin a new life. After all, I had a trade, and I knew of a friend in London, the great *modiste* Marie de Coulanges, an émigré like my mother, who would give me shelter. With the help of another friend, who shall for the moment be nameless, for if my husband knew of how he helped me, his life, too, might be at risk, I took with me as much of my husband's store of gold and cash as my friend could find to give me.

'So I ran away in the night, knowing full well that my disappearance would certainly cause my husband to be suspected of having murdered his wife. It may be wrong of me, but I gloried in the knowledge that I could make him suffer as I had suffered. Let everyone think that the Steepwood curse had struck again. This time, unlike my marriage to that monster—for that is what he is—I had made the right decision. You may imagine my surprise when, with my store of money and the help of my friend in London, my success as a *modiste* finally brought me to Bond Street. For the first time in my life I have felt both happy and safe.'

Athene nodded. She was well aware of the hardships which Louise had suffered as a dressmaker's apprentice, and was sorry to learn that they had been succeeded by the misery of her life as the Marchioness.

'You never told me,' she said at last. 'You should have come to me for help.'

Louise shook her head. 'Your own life was hard enough—as witness your present position. Your friendship and your letters in the long and difficult years of my apprenticeship kept me going, prevented me from falling into despair. Now I can repay you for that. I cannot deck you out as your figure and your beauty deserve, for the old baggage would be sure to wonder where such glory came from. What I can do is dress you with a modest elegance which will appeal to all those who possess real taste and can recognise it in others. The old cat will not appreciate the beauty of such a restrained toilette. Her own preference is for the garish, but fortunately, I have prevented her from overwhelming poor Emma with it.

'When we have finished our tea we shall go downstairs and I will begin the pleasant task of dressing you almost as you ought to be dressed. I see no reason why you should not end the Season with a husband of your own—if you can find a man who is both good and kind. I am hoping that Mrs T. will not sell poor little Emma to some monster with a title.'

Well, Adrian Kinloch was not a monster, but Athene had already secretly appropriated him for herself. She said hesitantly, 'You must know that I cannot pay you. Perhaps I could give you a little on account…'

'Nonsense!' exclaimed Louise robustly. 'You did not grasp what I was saying. Consider your trousseau—for that is what it is—as some small repayment for your many kindnesses.'

Appalled, Athene said, 'I don't deserve it.' She was thinking of her scheming over Adrian.

'Nonsense again, my love. Come, let us make a

beginning. I will brook no argument over this. I am your *modiste* now, and my word is law.'

Athene gave way as gracefully as she could. 'I will only agree if we can renew our old friendship as and when we can.'

'Granted,' said Louise, rising. Everything she did was done elegantly and matched the delicacy of her face and figure with its crown of fine golden hair. 'To celebrate it after we have decided on your new toilette, let us take a turn along Bond Street. One of the few things I miss about Steepwood Abbey is its fresh air and its glorious views. Not that there is much fresh air in Bond Street, but at least we shall be in the open, even if for only a short time.'

'Yes,' said Athene rising and following Louise— whom she must remember to call Madame Félice— 'There is very little for you to paint in London's dirty streets.'

The two young women spent a happy hour deciding on Athene's new clothes before putting on their bonnets and shawls and walking arm in arm down a street crowded with passers-by of all ages and sexes. Athene thought afterwards that it was the first happy day she had spent since alighting from the Tenisons' carriage which had brought her to London. She and Louise laughed and talked together as easily as though they had never been parted. When, at last, they did separate, Athene to return to the Tenisons and Louise to her shop, they both congratulated themselves on an afternoon well spent.

Athene would not have felt so happy if she had known that she had had a critical observer. Nick Cameron, who had just spent an afternoon at Jackson's boxing saloon, had been one of the passers-by. He had recognised not only her, but also her companion. A friend of his had recently pointed Madame Félice out to him in Hyde Park one day when she had been driven there in her open carriage.

'No one,' the friend had said coarsely, 'could convince me that that particular high-stepper isn't there for a man's taking.'

Nick had nodded back. He didn't care for loose talk about women in public—or in private for that matter—but he had secretly agreed.

So what was Miss Athene Filmer, the Tenisons' supposedly virtuous young companion, doing walking along a public thoroughfare engaging in animated conversation with someone who was the butt of all the fashionable young bucks and pinks who frequented London society? What price her virtue now?

He made an immediate resolution to test it.

CHAPTER THREE

'A masked ball,' exclaimed Mrs Tenison doubtfully. 'Are you sure that it would be quite the thing
for us to attend?'

'Not everyone who attends a *bal masqué* necessarily wears a mask—or more properly a domino, which
is the half-mask which used to be worn with a large
black cloak, but the cloak is not now obligatory,' explained Mr Tenison a trifle wearily. 'Besides, since
the Mortimers who are giving this ball are of the first
stare socially, we need have no fear that we shall be
compromising ourselves in any way by attending it.
Everyone who is anyone will be there.'

'Most of the cousinry in fact,' said Athene quietly.
She had rapidly learned that this word described the
majority of the leading aristocracy and gentry, all of
whom were more or less related to everyone else of
consequence in their world.

'Exactly,' said Mr Tenison.

Mrs Tenison said sharply, 'I do not see the point

of wearing a large cloak which covers one's toilette. I am glad to hear that its use is not necessary now.'

Emma offered, a trifle timidly, 'I suppose, Mama, that the notion was that the cloak makes it more difficult to identify who is wearing it.'

The fact that she was ready to challenge her mother a little when previously she had always been her abject slave in speech and behaviour amused Athene and pleased her papa. Separately they both saw it as a sign that going into society was beginning to have a liberating effect on her. Madame Félice's determination to design a dress to suit Emma's taste, rather than her mother's, had also had its influence on her.

Athene had already made up her mind to wear the gown which Madame had privately created for her. It was a dream of a thing in aquamarine silk so plainly, but so perfectly, cut that when Mrs Tenison first saw it she had no notion that it shrieked high-class in every line. Its only ornament was a tiny spray of silk forget-me-nots.

'You are not to wear any jewellery with it,' Louise had told Athene when she had tried it on.

'I haven't any,' said Athene, a trifle mournfully.

'All the better,' Louise had replied in her Madame Félice voice. 'Most women wear too much.'

'You don't regret leaving yours behind then?' asked Athene curiously.

'A little—but then I only had a little, and even so, I should never have worn everything at once like some women do!'

She handed Athene a tiny fan of the same colour as the forget-me-nots. 'That's a present from me to you, and when you make a grand marriage, which I am sure that you will, you must order all your clothes from me.'

Despite Mrs Tenison's failure to recognise Madame's handiwork, Athene knew that she looked her best when she walked a little behind Emma, whose own looks were enhanced by the pretty white gown which Madame had created for her.

Like Athene's it was too plain for her Mama's taste, but for the first time Emma was feeling happy to be going to a ball, since she had always considered herself to be monstrously over-dressed before.

'There they are, there's my beauty,' hissed Adrian to Nick.

They were watching the crowd making their way upstairs. The Tenisons' party, which included Lady Dunlop, who had given Athene's dress a long look, had not yet put on their masks, which were of the simplest kind. Adrian and Nick were wearing dominoes which had come from Venice and which possessed beaks like birds that covered their noses and made them harder to identify. They were not the only guests who were wearing more than the minimum required. Many, however, like Lady Dunlop, wore no mask at all.

Nick, after giving Athene a close examination— poor Emma was inspected by neither of them— thought, but did not tell Adrian, that the elegant gown which the lowly companion was wearing must also have been made for her by Madame Félice.

He was more intrigued by her than ever, dammit! If he had had to be attracted to a woman at all, why could he not have been dazzled by some perfectly respectable young miss of good family? Even if he had wanted to marry, which he didn't, he did not need to marry an heiress, for although he was by no means as rich as Adrian he was more comfortable—or warmer, as the money men had it—than most.

Instead he was lusting after a houri whom he was more than ever sure had set her sights on his cousin solely because of his rank and money. He reproached himself a little for being so angry about this. After all, were not the Tenisons doing exactly the same for their daughter by bringing her to London and to the marriage mart of high society? It was quite obvious that Miss Filmer had no parents wealthy enough to launch her into the *beau monde*.

So where had the money come from for the dress?—and why was Miss Filmer so friendly with a ladybird of dubious reputation, for his informant had also added that she must be financed by some man with money, since she had come from nowhere and had immediately opened her luxurious salon in the most expensive part of town. The current *on dit* was that only a rich protector could possibly explain *that*—the puzzle was: whoever could it be, since she was never seen in the company of a man?

Adrian chattered away all the time that Nick was

trying to solve his own puzzle. He was asking himself why, in the name of all that was holy, were the affairs of Miss Athene Filmer taking up so much of his time? Was it only because he did not want Adrian to be caught in a loveless marriage by a woman who was unsuitable? He shuddered reminiscently at the very thought.

Once he had thought to marry a girl whom he had believed to be kind and innocent: a girl with whom he had grown up and whom he had hoped to make his wife when his time at university was over. Instead…

At this point he gave up and concentrated instead on listening to his cousin. There was no point in raking over the unhappy past in a crowded ballroom— or anywhere else, for that matter. So instead, he gave Adrian the attention he deserved.

'I particularly wish to ask Athene to dance with me,' he was saying, 'but unfortunately, the Tenisons will expect me to ask Emma as soon as we meet, and not her companion. You could ask Athene first, while I take on Emma. After that it would not be odd for me to do the pretty and take pity on the companion for whom no one else will offer besides yourself. Provided, of course, that you have invited Emma on to the floor before I could ask her again. That way I would be able to have at least one dance with Athene without anyone thinking it odd.'

Nick was on the point of saying, 'Certainly not, I will not be party to such a deception,' when, to his astonishment, he heard himself saying, 'If that is what you wish, then I will oblige you. But just this once—and no more.'

What in the world was he thinking of? Had he not already made up his mind that he would never oblige Adrian in his pursuit of Athene, and here he was, doing that very thing!

On the other hand it would give him a splendid opportunity to try to provoke Athene into saying something which would give her little game away. Yes, that was it, that was why he was agreeing to help Adrian, and not because it would give him the opportunity to be alone with Athene.

Having comforted himself with this, he made a point of going over to the Tenisons in Adrian's wake and dutifully asking the scheming companion to join the dance with him. Not that he intended to take her on to the floor—by no means. He had a better plan than that, and one which might enable him to trump all of Pallas Athene's aces.

Athene, standing mute behind her charge, aware that more than one man had looked approvingly at Louise's creation, watched the cousins cross the ball-room towards their party. She recognised them immediately despite their masks, and watched Adrian bow and offer for Emma in the most gallant manner possible.

Emma blushed and allowed him to take her hand and lead her away. To Athene's great surprise Nicholas Cameron bowed in her direction and asked

in as pleasant a voice as he could muster, 'Do I collect
that you do not have a partner for this dance, Miss
Filmer? If so I would be honoured to take you on to
the floor.'

Athene offered him a small bow. 'It would be my
pleasure, too, sir.'

This statement was not entirely untruthful.
Something about Nick Cameron frightened her, but
she could not, in decency, refuse him, and if she were
honest she was beginning to find him strangely attractive. Besides, it was, after all a kind offer, for no
one would have expected him to squire an insignificant companion.

He was holding his hand out to her.

She took it.

Immediately the strong sensation which had surprised them before surprised them again. Nick, stifling
his own rapid response, led Athene towards the opposite side of the room, where a number of couples
were assembling for the dance and, more importantly,
where they were out of sight of the watching
Tenisons.

Instead of joining the dancers, however, he murmured softly, 'I know that this is meant to be an evening for pleasure, but you may not know that Lord
Mortimer has one of the finest libraries in England.
It even rivals that of Lord Holland. I wonder if you
would care to forgo the dance and join me in inspecting it. It is, I assure you, an opportunity not to be
missed.'

Athene hesitated before answering him. 'Etiquette would say, Mr Cameron, that I should not leave the dance floor to allow a young, unmarried man to take me, unescorted by an older woman, to visit a library—however innocent such an excursion might seem to be.'

Nick's eyes glittered behind his mask. That, and its eagle-like beak, gave him, for the briefest moment, the appearance of a bird of prey about to strike. The effect was so momentary that Athene wondered whether she had imagined it.

Her original reaction was, however, reinforced when he merely said, almost idly, 'The proprieties do trouble you then, Miss Filmer? I had begun to wonder if they did. May I assure you that you are perfectly safe with me, although whether I am safe from you is quite another matter! Our absence is unlikely to be noticed and I was doing you the honour of supposing you would relish the prospect of improving your education. I have no intention of destroying your reputation.'

Athene shivered and looked around her. His effect on her was so strong that she would have liked to run from him in order to save herself from the powerful feelings which overwhelmed her whenever she was with him. They were, however, in the open, as it were, and she could not create a scene which would ruin her—but not him. He was now gently urging her through the press around them until they arrived before a pair of double doors.

Desperately, she said, 'If I could be sure that I could trust you...'

'You may trust me absolutely,' he told her, opening one of the doors into the corridor and leading her, unresisting, through it. 'I shall be as honest as you always are, Miss Filmer. I respect, and fully understand, your reservations about joining me in the Mortimers' library and will behave like a perfect gentleman at all times.'

Reason informed her that if Mr Nicholas Cameron truly respected her he would not try to persuade her to break the conventions which ruled the lives of women of their class. Reason also said, in an even more convincing voice, might it not be useful to find out exactly why he dislikes you so much? For she was sure that he did dislike her, from the manner in which he always examined her with hooded eyes. A private conversation with him might enable her to discover why he did.

More than that, was he also sharing the peculiar sensations which coursed through her whenever he touched her? Or were they simply something odd which she was experiencing? It could not be, surely, that she found him attractive, since he was the exact opposite in appearance and behaviour of the imaginary heroes who had filled her daydreams since she was a small girl.

He did not look like Apollo, or any of the pictures of the Greek gods which she had often admired in the drawings in the great folios in Mr Tenison's library.

Nor was he soft-spoken, charming or worshipful to her when he talked to her: Adrian Kinloch's admiration of her was as patent as Nick Cameron's lack of it was. Adrian's appearance, too, resembled that of an Apollo come to earth.

Nick, by contrast, was similar to the swarthy, physically powerful and dominating Mars, the god of war, and in Shakespeare's words, 'like Mars he possessed an eye to threaten or command'. He was of the earth, earthy, and when he spoke to her his voice always sounded as though he were mocking her and all her doings. That he was clever was beyond a doubt, and in that, too, he did not resemble his handsome, feckless cousin.

All this swirled through Athene's mind while her Nemesis, for so she had begun to think of him, led her silently down a corridor lined with the busts of Roman emperors, and through another set of doors into the magnificent room which was Lord Mortimer's library.

He closed the doors behind them, and saying, 'At last,' turned to face her.

'Now, Miss Filmer,' he began, 'we may start to know one another. Tell me, I do beg of you, by what means you have come to possess an evening gown made for you by London's leading *modiste,* when I understand that you're a penniless young lady brought into society in order to chaperon the Tenisons' timid young miss. Penniless young ladies cannot afford Madame Félice's prices.'

Her face paling, Athene swung away from him to wrench at the handles of the double doors. Over her shoulder she said to him in as fierce a voice as she could summon up, 'No! I shall not answer you. I was mistaken to agree to accompany you here. You persuaded me to do so under false pretences, and I demand that you return me at once to the ballroom. I want no more of you, or your lying insinuations.'

Nick leaned back against one of the pillars which supported a ceiling on which the god Jupiter was carrying off Europa.

'By no means,' he drawled. 'I merely asked you a question which many will be asking. My own curiosity was piqued by seeing you in Bond Street in the company of a mysterious woman who is as notorious for her lack of morals as for the superb gowns which she designs and sells. How came you to know her, my provincial butterfly? What price your innocence if you are her friend and confidante?'

Athene stared back at him, and said, still fierce, 'That is my business, sir, and none of yours. You may ask your questions, but I shall not answer them.'

She had the doors open now and was about to leave when Nick caught her by the shoulders and swung her round to face him before he released her. In that brief moment she felt the full power of his rough strength.

'By God, madam, you *will* answer me, for my cousin's business is mine, and you have made him yours. He thinks and talks of nothing else but you,

and deludes that poor child and her parents into believing that she is the one he is interested in. What's
your little game, madam? Or is it a big one? Pray do
not tell me that you have fallen desperately in love
with him. You are a clever woman but you cannot
bam me.'

Athene's answer was as fierce as his question. 'I
have no wish to bam you, sir, nor anyone else. It is
you who have bammed *me* by luring me hither on
pretence of inspecting Lord Mortimer's library in order to treat me as though you were a hanging judge
and I were a convicted criminal in your court.'

Nick was full of a reluctant admiration for her
fierce spirit, which had transformed her face so that
she looked lovelier than ever. It was taking him all
his strength of will not to fall upon her, to take her
into his arms. Instead he continued to admonish her,
reminding himself that, on the evidence, he was right
to do so.

'Oh, madam, I think you would do well in a wor-
thier cause than that on which you are embarked. The
goddess after whom you were named could then be
proud of you. Alas, I cannot believe that you are being honest with me—or with your employers—over
your pursuit of my cousin or the origin of the clothes
which you are wearing.'

'I repeat, sir. It is no business of yours who makes
my clothes, any more than I have the right to choose
your tailor and boot-maker. If I were to assume that
right I should make sure that you would look less like

an unmade bed and more like the cousin of one of society's finest beaux—for whom I happen to have formed a *tendre!*'

'Oh, brave,' was his answer to that. 'Nevertheless, I know full well that you are not telling me the truth so far as your feelings for my cousin are concerned— and I intend to prove that I am right.'

Athene, who had been ready to leave, and to return to the ballroom alone—and damn the consequences— made the mistake of saying, 'Indeed, and how *do* you intend to prove that?'

'Like this,' he said, and before she could stop him he had his arms around her and his mouth on hers. His desire for her, increased by her fiery resistance, had completely overcome his discretion, and worse than that—his honour.

Athene had never been kissed before, other than by her mother, and certainly never by a man. Her first impulse was to pull away from him, but the sensations which had previously run through her when they had simply touched hands now overwhelmed her so much that her power to resist the attraction which lay be-tween them was as lost as his.

It was Nick who ended their first passionate em-brace—and solely because reason told him that they must return to the ballroom before the dance ended and their absence was noticed.

'Now, madam,' he said, drawing back and sardon-ically registering her dazed expression, so different from the picture of dislike which she had been show-

ing him only a moment before. 'Now, tell me after
that that it is my cousin who engages your loving
admiration—unless, of course, you respond to all men
so enthusiastically when they kiss you!'

Athene's dream of desire was broken immediately.
'Oh, you are detestable,' she exclaimed. 'Take me
back to the ballroom, at once, and never speak to me
again. You promised that you would behave like a
perfect gentleman and yet you immediately broke
your word. How can I ever trust you again?'

What in the world could he say to that? For it was
the truth, was it not? He could scarcely tell her that
alone with him she had proved by her mere presence—and not because she had encouraged him—to
be temptation itself.

'No,' he said, his voice sober. 'I cannot deny that
I have behaved badly, and I must ask you to forgive
me for my ungentlemanly conduct, but consider…'

'No, sir, I will consider nothing, nor will I forgive
you. I shall immediately return to the ballroom and
you must do as you please, since nothing you can do
would please me. Had you done as you had promised
I might have enjoyed inspecting Lord Mortimer's library with you, but, as it is…'

As it was, Athene was as good as her word. She
was through the door and along the corridor before
Nick started after her. He was the victim of a strange
mixture of conflicting emotions. On the one hand he
suspected her honesty more than ever since she had,
in effect, denied nothing. On the other hand he could

not but admire her fighting spirit. The phrase she had thrown at him reverberated in his head—you would look less like an unmade bed—and had him smiling at it ruefully.

Oh, yes, she had a way with words, had Miss Athene Filmer. It was like arguing with a leading lawyer in the courts at the Old Bailey, so quick was she to quibble at *his* every word. Nevertheless his own honour demanded that she did not return alone to the ballroom to be quizzed by every idle gossip in society.

He need not have worried. He rejoined her at its entrance to discover that the crowd was all agog over the latest public indiscretion of Lord Byron and Lady Caroline Lamb. Consequently the adventures—or misadventures—of a country miss were hardly likely to attract their attention away from that salacious piece of gossip.

All eyes were upon the Lady and her flushed face. She had apparently started a blazing argument with M'lord on the edge of the dance floor—to which he had replied by limping out of the ballroom, leaving the spectators and the dancers all agog. By morning the *on dits* would be flying around London!

Only Mrs Tenison said crossly to Athene when she reached her station behind her, 'Wherever have you been? I missed seeing you in the dance, and then the commotion which Lady Caroline caused was such that I could not even watch Emma and Lord Kinloch! If Lady Caroline were my daughter I would make it my business to see that she did not disgrace herself in public. They say that her husband was gaming in one of the salons and could not be troubled to come and control her. It was left to her mother to pick up the pieces and not, I understand, for the first time.'

Naturally Athene could not express her relief that Lady Caroline's behaviour had managed to prevent her own misadventure from becoming public knowledge. Emma and Adrian's return to the family party meant that she had no need to reply to Mrs Tenison's petulance, since Emma's mother immediately began to tell Adrian that she had brought her daughter up properly so that she would never disgrace her husband and family in public.

'Quite so, and I compliment you,' replied Adrian tactfully. He spoilt this piece of flattery by adding, 'Miss Emma is a very unicorn of virtue, is she not?'

All three Tenisons and Athene stared at him when he came out with this unlikely statement. Nick, who had also joined the party, muttered in an undertone to his cousin, 'I think that you meant paragon there, Adrian.'

'Oh, did I?' exclaimed Adrian innocently. 'Forgive me, Miss Emma. I fear I neglected my books when I was a lad, but Nick is quite the scholar and always rescues me.'

Athene said as sweetly as she could, giving Nick a sideways basilisk stare, 'Oh, I think I like unicorn better than paragon, Lord Kinloch, seeing that the unicorn is the symbol of virtue.'

This earned *her* two sideways looks: one from Mr Tenison and the other from Nick, but Adrian, brightening up after his *faux pas,* said in his cheerful inconsequential way, 'Is that so, Miss Filmer? I must remember that in future, it could be useful in conversation. I am most grateful to you.'

He ended by giving her another sideways look in which adoration and admiration were equally mixed.

Mr Tenison made a muffled sound which could have been understood as a strangled cough rather than the strangled laugh it actually was. Nick said dourly, 'Miss Filmer's grasp of language is unequalled. She would make an excellent writer—all she needs to begin is a first-rate plot—but perhaps she has thought of one already.'

Athene was saved from having to answer this two-edged compliment by Mr Tenison who said jovially—which was in itself remarkable, for he was by no means a jovial man—'May I suggest that we repair to the supper-room? Both dancing and watching others dance are dry work, and a refreshing drink would do us all the world of good.'

It was Athene's turn to stifle a strangled laugh. She had long been aware that Mr Tenison was more *au fait* with the realities of what was going on around him than either his wife, his daughter, or his friends. He was one of life's observers and the undertones of the recent bout of conversation were apparently as plain to him as they were to her.

Emma, looking worshipfully up at Adrian, who had

eyes only for Athene, said gently, 'I like being called a unicorn. I think that they are splendid creatures, but I always think of myself as more of a mouse,' she ended, a trifle mournfully.

For the first time Adrian took a good look at her. 'Certainly not, Miss Emma. There is nothing of the mouse about you. I would rather say that you resembled a...' He had begun his sentence carelessly and could not think how to end it.

Inspiration struck. 'A robin, perhaps. I think that they are jolly little birds, bright-eyed and hopping merrily about. Is not that so, Nick?'

'Oh, indeed,' said his cousin. 'They also have the advantage of not being showy birds, like some, but they do have a rare integrity,' and he bowed in Emma's direction.

Discomposed, she coloured, but retained enough *savoir-faire* to say simply, 'I think that you both over-compliment me—but, yes, I think that I like being called a robin.'

Mrs Tenison was not sure that she approved of Emma being called a robin, but her husband was pleased. At least Lord Kinloch had had the goodness to look properly at his daughter for once instead of mooning after her companion. It was not that he disliked the thought of Athene attracting the noble lord, but he did not approve of M'lord using Emma as a diversion.

It was as plain to him as it was to Nick that Athene and Adrian were not suited to one another. M'lord would bore her to tears in a week if they married, and he would not know what to say to her when the week was up. In the long run he would probably prefer someone who would worship him, rather than that it would be he who would have to do the worshipping. Now someone like young Cameron would be a far better bet for Athene—*they* would never run out of conversation, that was for sure.

The pity was that young people never quite knew who it was that they ought to be running after. Usually they hankered after the moon when a shy star would be much better for them. He took his wife's arm to prevent her from saying something unwise, and watched with some amusement Nick Cameron hastily annex Athene so that Kinloch was left to escort Emma.

He also knew that, in the usual way of things, the cousins were not likely to ask poor Athene Filmer to marry them since she possessed neither family nor money, but at least she would have had a few evenings' admiration from the pair of them, even if it came to nothing.

Neither he, nor any of his party, noticed that, as in Bond Street with Nick Cameron, Athene had attracted a man's attention.

A middle-aged nobleman with a handsome face full of character stood at a little distance from them. Another gentleman who was somewhat younger was beside him. As Athene's party passed him the nobleman said abruptly to his companion, 'Have you any notion who the beauty on the arm of young Cameron might be?'

'None, Duke, but I can find out for you. I would have thought, though, that she is a trifle young for your taste.'

'As to that, Tupman,' said the Duke of Inglesham coldly, 'since my wife died I have had no taste at all for women, either young or old. But this particular child interests me because she greatly resembles someone whom I knew years ago when I was a green boy. I merely wondered whether she was related to her.'

Now, this was intriguing. The Duke's reputation so far as women were concerned was spotless, despite the fact that he had married a shrew who had led him an unholy dance before she had expired suddenly from a syncope brought on by a fit of raging temper.

'Leave it to me,' Tupman said. 'I promise to be discreet. They are walking to the supper room. I know Cameron and I can have a quiet word with him there about his companion.'

The Duke sighed. 'As you please,' he said with apparent indifference. The likeness which he thought that he had seen had moved him greatly, but he did not wish Tupman to know that.

Nick, Adrian and Mr Tenison were standing at the supper table, having found a quiet corner for the ladies to seat themselves. Nick was moving away from his companions when he saw that wretched gossip, Tupman, coming towards him holding a plate of food and a glass of wine.

'Hello, Cameron, thought it was you I saw in the distance. Who was the beauty you had on your arm? You always seem to be able to corner them, you dog, I wonder how you do it.'

Nick returned stiffly, 'That was Miss Athene Filmer. She is by way of being the companion of Miss Emma Tenison.'

'Oho, the Northamptonshire heiress? A little backward in coming forward is she not, despite all the money? Is Miss Filmer an heiress, too?'

'Not that I know of, but we haven't discussed that yet. She and the Tenisons are very recent acquaintances.'

'And does she hail from the wilds, too? You must introduce me later.'

'Indeed,' said Nick, desperate to get away before Adrian joined them and began to enlarge on Athene's merits, thus giving the vacuous beau who was quizzing him fuel for more gossip to spread around society. 'You will forgive me if I leave you. I must do my duty by my friends.'

He left Tupman behind as quickly as he could. That gentleman stared after him in surprise. Nick Cameron had a reputation for being abrupt, but he was seldom as curt as that. Now what fly was buzzing round his head to make him so exceedingly testy? It might be a good idea to find out.

In the meantime he would take Miss Filmer's name

back to Inglesham and watch his reaction when he told it to him.

He was to be disappointed. Inglesham was as calm and collected as ever, and quite indifferent when he was told of the beauty's name and origins.

'From Northamptonshire, you say. Hmm, perhaps I was deceived over the likeness. Nevertheless, accept my thanks for your kindness.'

One person not deceived was Nick Cameron. Some instinct—an instinct which had served him well before—had him watching Tupman return to the Duke and engage him in urgent conversation the moment he reached him.

Now why, in the name of wonder, should Inglesham be interested in Athene Filmer? For the same instinct told him that Tupman was reporting back about her to the man he was toadying to. The toadying was not a surprise—Tupman toadied to everyone great—but that Inglesham should encourage it was.

Another surprise, although when Nick thought about it later it was not a surprise at all, was that Inglesham was not the only person to be interested in Athene. Every male eye in the room seemed to have noticed that the Tenisons had brought an unknown beauty with them. Athene, without doing anything but be her own lovely self, had made the impression on society which she had intended when she had left Northamptonshire.

Louise's dress had helped her, of course.

The result of this turn-about was that Adrian's cunning ploy to ensure that, after supper, he had a dance with Athene without offending the Tenisons, came to nothing!

Nick and he arrived to discover that Athene and Emma were now promised to other interested men for the rest of the evening. Fortunately for Emma, those who arrived to claim Athene's hand and were disappointed turned their attention to her charge, who found that, reflected in Athene's glory, she was as much in demand as any other débutante in the room.

Mrs Tenison wailed to her husband when Nick and Adrian discovered that both girls were being led on to the floor by other young hopefuls, 'Whatever has come over everyone, Mr Tenison? Why should Athene become such a centre of interest? She is a nobody, and her dress is modest, to say the least.'

'But very charming, and her deportment is incomparable. On the other hand, Emma is in looks tonight, and is having her share of admiration.'

Mrs Tenison made a face. Her husband interpreted it correctly. He said gently, 'Do not envy Athene her evening of glory, my dear. Young men will cheerfully dance with her, but once they know of her lack of fortune, they will never offer for her. Emma, on the other hand, is a double prize—looks *and* money. Given time she will blossom in these surroundings, Mrs Tenison, be sure of that. No, grudge poor Athene nothing.'

'So long as Filmer does not get above herself,' his wife sniffed.

Filmer, as Mrs Tenison preferred to call her, was enjoying herself. She was not only basking in male admiration, but she was also showing Nick Cameron that she was attractive to other men besides his cousin.

If these other men did not particularly attract her as much as Nick Cameron did, then he was not to know that. Indeed, he must never know it. Adrian Kinloch was still her goal. With his wealth and power in society he could, in marrying her, give her everything which her mother deserved, and if she had to sacrifice something to marry him, then so be it.

She saw, moving through the arabesques of the dance, that he was watching her with sad eyes. The expression on Nick Cameron's face was unreadable.

Oh, the evening had been a triumph, no doubt of it. Adrian, seeing her admired by others, would admire her the more.

So, why did she feel so empty?

CHAPTER FOUR

'This arrived for you by a special messenger a few moments ago, Miss Filmer. He did not wait for an answer.'

The Tenisons' butler handed Athene a letter when she walked into the entrance hall on the way to enjoying a very late breakfast the morning after the Mortimers' ball.

The servants never knew quite what to make of her. She always behaved with the utmost propriety, knew her place—which was somewhere between them and the Tenisons—but they also knew that it was whispered that there was some mystery attached to her widowed mother.

That no one appeared to know what exactly what the mystery consisted of simply made it more mysterious than ever! Mrs Filmer had certainly arrived out of nowhere and she appeared to possess no relations, for none had ever been seen visiting her.

Athene duly thanked the butler before retiring to

the drawing-room to read her letter. She had no wish to be cross-questioned by Mrs Tenison about its origin and its contents. The only person she knew in London who might send her one was Madame Félice, and the less her domineering employer knew about her friendship with Louise, the better.

The note was short. It simply said: 'Some remarkable news has reached me. It may also have reached you by now. I need to discuss the meaning of it, and its possible consequences for me, with someone whom I can trust, and you are the only person in London I can safely call friend. I beg of you to visit me as soon as you can find the time to do so. MF.'

Athene crumpled the letter in her hand. Whatever could have happened to have resulted in such a *cri de coeur*? She would find her way to Bond Street that very afternoon, for if she was the only person Louise could trust, then the reverse was true. Louise was her only trustworthy friend and they must present a united front to an unkind world.

She walked into breakfast shortly before Mr Tenison, who arrived in a state of agitation: a state which was unusual for him. He was carrying a letter both larger and longer than her own.

'My dears,' he said, and his voice was as agitated as his manner. 'I have had some disturbing news from home. I thought that it would be better for me to inform you of it in private before you read about it in the public prints. It is sure to be in the *Morning Post* either today or tomorrow. Lawyer Simpkin tells me as a matter of urgency, seeing that I was having some contentious legal discussions with him, that the Marquis of Sywell was found dead in his bedroom at the Abbey several days ago. He had been brutally murdered by some person, or persons, unknown.'

Mrs Tenison gave a great moan. 'Another assassination,' she exclaimed. 'It is not long since the poor Prime Minister, Mr Spencer Perceval, was shot by that madman, Bellingham. We are none of us safe,' and she dabbed her handkerchief to her eyes to express her grief.

'Not that I ever liked the man,' she added, recovering as suddenly as she had been overcome. 'The Marquis, I mean, not Mr Perceval. We are surely not expected to go into mourning for him. He was only a neighbour, not a relative.'

'To be truthful,' said Mr Tenison, 'I can't imagine anyone who will mourn him. He was the most disagreeable of men. On the other hand that does not mean that I wished him dead.'

'The curse,' said Emma faintly. 'The Steepwood curse has worked again. First the Marchioness disappears and now the Marquis is murdered. Perhaps the same person killed them both.'

Athene, handing Emma her handkerchief, since Emma appeared to have lost hers and was paying the curse, rather than the Marquis, the respect of tears, murmured, 'That would be a great leap in logic. Does your letter say, sir, whom the authorities might suspect?'

Mr Tenison, surveying his tearful womenfolk and grateful for Athene's sturdy common-sense, answered her immediately, 'No. It appears to be as great a mystery as his wife's disappearance. The trouble is, I suppose, that there are many who had words with him—as I did—but one cannot assume that that necessarily means that one of us rid the world of him.'

Athene nodded. She thought that she now knew of what Louise was writing in her letter and why she needed to speak to someone straight away. She also thought that she ought to burn the letter immediately. One other thing was certain: the Marquis's murder would form the subject of gossip and conversation for at least a week before some other remarkable news superseded it. After all, who spoke of the late Prime Minister now?

'Sywell, murdered. I can't say that I'm surprised. Especially after having read the saucy squib about him that's been circulating recently.'

Nick Cameron and Adrian had just encountered George Tupman in Bond Street on the way to Jackson's boxing saloon. He had stopped them in order to pass on the news which had just arrived in a letter from his brother who lived near Steepwood Abbey.

'What saucy squib are you referring to, Tupman?' asked Nick.

'Oh, haven't you come across it? I suppose since you arrived in London some little time after it first surfaced, you missed all the original excitement it caused. It's a satire about Sywell, entitled *The Wicked Marquis*—he's called Rapeall in the book and half society is pilloried in it. It was published by one of those low fellows who make money out of such things, and it's been passed from hand to hand. If half of what was in it is true, most of the ton had cause to finish him off. The news of his death is sure to be in the *Morning Post* tomorrow,' he finished importantly. 'I thought that you'd like to be the first in the know.'

'Of all the many people who disliked or feared him,' offered Nick, 'which one would you put money on as the murderer, Tupman, if asked to place a bet?'

Tupman shrugged. 'Possibly a servant—or a Luddite, or some other malcontent. I can't imagine one of us doing such a thing. A bit extreme, that!'

Adrian said, 'I never met him. Was he as bad as the squib says? By the by, I should like to read it some time, particularly if I'm in it.'

'Worse, one might suppose,' said Nick briefly. 'I only had the bad luck to encounter him once. He was beating some wretched footman nearly senseless for some imaginary breach of etiquette. It took me all my self-command not to wrench the whip from him and use it on his sides. I was only a lad, then, and beating Marquises was a bit above my touch. It would be different now.'

'They say it's the Steepwood Abbey curse working again,' said Tupman, his eyes as round as Emma's.

'It's mentioned in the squib. You may borrow my copy of it, Kinloch, but only if you'll promise to return it. And no, you're not in it, and you should be pleased. Those who are have been given unkind names and made fun of.'

Adrian was not sure that he was happy about being left out, even if he would have been made fun of if he had been mentioned.

'So, it's true that there's a curse on Steepwood,' he finally said.

'They always come out with some sort of nonsense about curses when there's a mysterious death,' said Nick robustly. 'Who believes in them these days?'

'I do,' said Adrian. 'There are lots of them in our family history. Scotland is full of curses, Nick, you should know that.'

Nick shrugged his shoulders. He thanked Tupman for his news and the cousins walked on—in time to see Athene entering Madame Félice's shop.

'I say,' exclaimed Adrian. 'Wasn't that Athene? What splendid luck! We can make an excuse to go in. It will give me a chance to talk to her.'

'Depending on which famous gossip is also patronising Madame, it might be a splendid chance to have someone start to chatter about you and her after a fashion you might not like,' said Nick sensibly. 'Besides, what is she doing there? She can't afford Madame's prices—which is why it's a small mystery how she came to be wearing one of Madame's creations last night.'

'Are you sure she was?' said Adrian doubtfully. 'It didn't seem very up to snuff to me, rather ordinary, in fact. Can't see where the mystery comes in.'

Nick couldn't help thinking that his cousin's lack of judgement over Athene's turn-out was yet one more reason why the pair of them would never suit. Adrian's taste ran to the gaudy—he couldn't see Athene standing for that.

'I still say that you wouldn't be best advised to enter such a female paradise without any real reason for doing so.'

'Oh, very well,' scowled Adrian, 'you're always a wet blanket, Nick, but...'

'But I'm usually right,' said Nick, taking his cousin's arm and steering him away from temptation.

Inside the shop Louise rapidly found an excuse to send Athene to the workroom at the back, and having disposed of her current customer she took her upstairs again, leaving word that she was not to be disturbed for at least the next half-hour.

Instead of serving tea, she walked to a sideboard where a decanter of Madeira and some elegant cut-glass goblets stood. She half-filled two of them before handing one to Athene saying, 'Drink this. I fear that you will need it before I have finished.'

Her lovely composure, which Athene had always admired, appeared to have deserted her. She took a small swallow, shuddered and put her glass down.

'To business. I must not waste your time. I had a

letter from a confidential friend in Steepwood: the friend who helped me to escape. It contained some shocking news. I never had reason to care for my husband after I discovered how much he had deceived me into marrying him by pretending that he was madly in love with me, but I would not have wished on him what has actually occurred.'

She was, unknowingly, echoing everyone's epitaph for the dead man when the news was broken to them.

'He has been found in his bedroom, foully and brutally murdered. By whom is a mystery. It seems that he had sent all the servants away including Solomon Burneck, his butler-cum-valet, so he was alone in that great barracks of a place. If it were not for that, poor Solomon might have been a logical suspect, for there appears to be little doubt that he was Sywell's illegitimate son, and was very badly treated by him— giving him a good motive for murder.'

She paused before going on. 'He had been slashed to death with his own razor after what seems to have been a prolonged struggle. There was blood everywhere. Naturally, the question of my own disappearance has been raised again, although I gather from my informant that the nature of his death meant that no woman could have killed him. Some suspicion appears to have fallen on Lord Yardley—he had had yet another public and violent quarrel with Sywell, not long before. One problem for those trying to discover who might have killed him is that he quarrelled so violently with so many people—most of whom might have wished him dead.'

'Yes,' agreed Athene. 'I know that he and Mr Tenison were at odds, but he seems to me to be a most unlikely murderer—besides he has not left London since we arrived here in mid-April.'

'There is something else which you ought to know,' continued Louise. 'My informant told me that the authorities are beginning another urgent search for the missing Marchioness. It is thought that there is a possibility that she might have paid someone to murder Sywell because she would not be able to kill him herself. You understand now why I have sent for you.'

'They surely could not possibly suspect you,' said Athene numbly. 'No one who knew you could think you capable of ordering him to be murdered.'

'Ah, but who did know me—apart from you?' said Louise wearily. 'Very few people ever met me. Once I married Sywell I was kept almost a prisoner, leaving the Abbey only to roam its grounds. Before that I was a humble seamstress with few friends and none of them—apart from yourself—from Steepwood. Besides, I do not wish to be found—not even to prove that I could not have murdered him. That part of my life is over and done with. I made a mistake when I married the wretch and I have already paid dearly enough for it. Sadly, I might not have done so, except that my guardian, John Hanslope, thought that it might be a good thing for me.'

'But why should they think that the Earl of Yardley might have murdered him?' asked Athene, a little bewildered. 'That seems to me as preposterous as supposing that you might have connived at it. I only met him once, but he seemed to be a quiet man, most respectable in his ways—quite unlike the Marquis.'

'That is how he is now,' explained Louise, 'but he was not always so. Sywell used to laugh about him to me when he was drunk. It seems—if my late husband can be believed—that in his youth, before he inherited the title, he was as wild as Sywell was. They were part of a set, which included the then Earl of Yardley, which gambled, drank and ran after disreputable women. Sywell boasted that he had won Steepwood Abbey and all the Yardley estates from the Earl in a long gambling session which lasted for days. It had been the family home of the Yardleys for generations.

'The worst thing was that Sywell also boasted to me that he had cheated the Earl, and that when the Earl had lost everything he blew his brains out on the spot. He always laughed when he got to that part of his horrible story—he told it to me many times because he was proud of his trickery, not ashamed of it.'

Athene said faintly, 'I had heard something of this. My mother never spoke of it. She hated gossip, so it came to me in bits and pieces from giggling girls at Mrs Guarding's. But it all happened long ago and the present Earl has made a great fortune for himself in

India, and has bought his own estate, so why should he want to kill the Marquis—who has impoverished himself by his own wicked folly—even to get Yardley land back again?'

'Agreed,' said Louise, 'and this is why I wished to speak to you. You are so common-sensical and ask all the right questions. On the other hand, it seems to me that most men do not behave very common-sensically when their money or their honour is at stake, particularly when they are drunk. We can only guess why Lord Yardley should quarrel with the Marquis after all these years, and must guess again as to whether that quarrel led to Sywell's death.'

Athene was thoughtful. 'It's like one of those wooden puzzles where you are given the individual counties of England as separate pieces and have to put them together to make the complete map,' she said, at last. 'It's hard enough to do that when you have all the pieces—if you don't, it's almost impossible.'

'True enough, and really all that concerns me is that neither of us should say or do anything which might reveal that *I* am Sywell's runaway wife. If anyone asks how we came to be friends we must be able to say something convincing which will mislead them completely—but which, alas, will not be truthful.'

The two girls—for they were little more—looked at one another ruefully until Athene said, with a sad laugh, 'If I were writing Minerva Press novels I might

be able to come up with a thundering lie to which no
one could find an objection, but as it is…'

'As it is, I am as stumped as you are,' confessed
Louise. 'I have told so many lies to account for how
I happen to be here in Bond Street, under a false
name, that I have quite run out of invention.'

'How about this,' said Athene, furrowing her brow,
and thinking hard before speaking. 'I had a French
governess for a short time, as you doubtless know.
We could say that she had a little sister—you—who
visited us for a short holiday once, and that when I
came to your salon with the Tenisons I recognised
you immediately as that child grown up, but said
nothing because it is no business of theirs.'

Her own ability to concoct a fairy-tale appalled
her—particularly since she could hear Nick
Cameron's sardonic voice saying, 'What a practised
liar and schemer you are, Athene, nearly as devious
as the goddess whose name you bear.'

She silenced the voice by listening to Louise's
praise of her explanation. 'That should suffice,' she
said, 'not that I think that anyone will track me down,
you understand, but there is always a remote possibility. One thing I have learned is that after the pre-
liminary lie one must keep the rest of the story simple.
Too many involved explanations can lead to trouble.'

Athene kissed Louise's sad face impulsively. 'Oh,
what a horrid world it is when poor girls like us are
driven to such extremes in order to survive.'

She was thinking not only of Louise, but of herself,

compelled to make her own way in the marriage market because her mother was unable to scheme for her. Even so, she now knew that she was in a better situation than Louise had ever been. Louise had had no one to introduce her into society, and the man who she had thought was her saviour had turned out to be a monster.

Louise, watching Athene's face change, wondered for the first time whether she ought to tell her friend the whole truth about her disputed origins. Alas, she knew only too well that Athene needed to be single-minded to survive herself, and to burden her with her own sad tale would help neither of them.

Perhaps that story could better be told on another day, when the news of the Marquis's horrible death had had time to sink in.

In the meantime all that was left to the pair of them was to finish off their glasses of Madeira and talk reminiscently of days gone by in order to forget the trying present.

'Dead! Goodness gracious—which one of his many enemies finally gave *him* the *coup de grâce?*' This comment, by a lady, was one of the kindest—and most repeatable—which the Marquis of Sywell's brutal death provoked in society. Worse, wherever one went, if the Earl of Yardley's heir was present, hushed whispers about his father's possible involvement in the murder followed him around.

Marcus, Viscount Angmering, was always easy to

identify. He was a well-built man with, like Nick Cameron, a strong, rather than a handsome face. He had a crown of unruly and bright red-gold hair which flamed like a beacon. On top of that he was of a practical turn and could never be troubled, despite his wealth, to play the society fop.

'The worst of it is,' he was confiding to Nick and Adrian one afternoon in Hyde Park, 'is that it is rather as though I have a strange disease which everyone knows about, but will not speak of. Those in society whom I most dislike behave towards me as though I am about to pass it on to them and the ones whom I do like speak to me with ill-disguised and heavy sympathy! The last person I would ever suspect of murder is my father—but that's hardly evidence is it? Just proof that I'm a dutiful son after all!'

'True, and there aren't many of them about these days,' agreed Nick, while Adrian, taking poor Marcus Angmering literally, asked anxiously, 'You haven't really got a strange disease, Angmering, have you?'

He was quite unable to understand why Nick and Marcus both began to laugh uncontrollably.

Marcus said, wiping his eyes, 'You're a good fellow, Kinloch, and I wouldn't risk your health by bamming you. No, I'm in fine fettle: it's just that my temper has grown rather short since the news of Sywell's murder arrived in town and started everyone gibbering nonsense at me.'

'Oh, splendid,' said Adrian, relieved, and then, 'I don't mean by that that I approve of Sywell's being killed—even though he did rather ask for it by the way he went on. I've just read that jolly tale about him, *The Wicked Marquis*. Nick says that lots of the fellows are in it. No, I'm relieved to learn that you're in good health. Sywell gave us all a bad name you know, helped those awful Radical fellows to tell lies about the House of Lords. Perhaps they'll shut up now he's gone.'

'Doubt it,' said Nick and Marcus together. Marcus added in a more sober tone, 'The oddest thing is that it seems that Sywell's manner of death was exactly like that in the book.'

'All covered in blood from being finished off with a razor,' exclaimed the entranced Adrian.

'Exactly,' replied Marcus. 'Either it's the most extraordinary coincidence, particularly since the book was written when Sywell was in good health—or relatively good health,' he rapidly amended, '—or the book suggested to the murderer the way to dispose of him.'

All three men reflected in their different fashion on Sywell's horrid end, before Nick decided to change the subject by taking advantage of Marcus's coming over to them by asking him if he knew the Tenisons of Steep Ride in Northamptonshire.

'Seeing that your family comes from Steepwood, Angmering, I thought that you might have met them. They are in London at present: their daughter is to be presented at Court.'

'Um, Tenison?' said Marcus thoughtfully. 'Yes, I

was introduced to him at the Assembly Rooms in Abbot Quincey when I was last there. Solid sort of fellow—a bit of a scholar. Had a chat with him about the history of the Abbey before my family owned it. M'father thought him a sound man, too. I can just about remember the daughter. A little thing, very silent—had one of those dominant mamas.'

'Had she a companion with her then?' asked Nick as though the question were an afterthought.

'Not that I remember. Who does remember companions, though?'

Adrian, who had been listening with half an ear, exclaimed rather testily, 'You'd remember this one if you'd ever met her, Angmering. She's a rare beauty, puts the little Tenison into the shade without even trying. Comes from the same part of the world.'

Neither Nick nor Marcus had ever seen Adrian so interested in anyone or anything before. Indignation at a possible slight to Athene poured out of him.

'What's the name of this paragon, Kinloch?—for paragon she must be to have engaged your interest— thought your taste ran to ladybirds.'

'Look here, Angmering, Miss Athene Filmer is no ladybird, she's a good girl, does her duty by the little Tenison, helps to bring her on, doesn't she, Nick?'

'One might think so,' said Nick noncommittally.

'Filmer,' mused Marcus. 'Can't say I remember a Filmer, and if she made such an impression on you, Kinloch, I'm sure I should have taken more than a passing interest in her if I'd met her.'

'Well,' said Adrian, still belligerent, 'you've a splendid opportunity to get to know her. I was hoping that the Tenisons would visit the park this afternoon, seeing that the weather is so splendid, and here they are. I shall persuade Miss Emma's mama and papa that it might be an excellent notion for her and her companion to leave their carriage and take a stroll with us so that you can judge her for yourself. After that I'm sure that you will agree with me that all companions are not elderly hags.'

He strode towards the Tenisons' open landau, leaving Marcus staring after him.

'I say, Cameron, what in the world has come over Kinloch? Surely he's not fallen head over heels in love with a lowly companion of all people? I would have thought he'd be the last man to do anything so odd. Not that he carries much weight in the attic, but I wouldn't have thought him as light as that!'

Nick, to his eternal astonishment, found himself defending Athene.

'You haven't seen the companion, Marcus. She is rather remarkable—and clever, too.'

'Clever! Then what in Hades do she and Kinloch find to talk about?'

Nick began to laugh. He'd forgotten what a downright fellow Angmering was, as downright as himself, in fact. And he had just put a blunt finger on Nick's own reservations about a marriage between Adrian and Athene.

He had no time to make a comment on these lines

to Marcus, since that nobleman was giving a whistle at the sight of Adrian—a young woman on each arm—striding proudly towards them.

'Good Gad, I see what he means. The little one has come on a bit since I last saw her, though. She's more than passable now, in fact, a pretty little thing. But the companion—she's a stunner and no mistake!'

Nick looked sourly at his old friend. What! This was the outside of enough! Was Pallas Athene on the way to getting yet another admirer! What, would the line stretch out to the crack of doom, as Shakespeare had it in *Macbeth*?

Marcus bowed deeply to both young women when Adrian introduced them.

'Delighted to meet you, ladies. What a lucky fellow you are, Kinloch! A belle on each arm. You told me before you went over to collect them that you were bringing me a pair of beauties, and you had the right of it.'

Emma blushed—charmingly—the days when she was overwhelmed by such praise were over. Athene said, 'You flatter us, m'lord.'

'No m'lords, Miss Filmer. I am Angmering to you—and also to Miss Emma, whom I remember meeting last Christmas in the Assembly Rooms at Abbot Quincey.'

'You honour me by remembering me, Angmering,' said Emma shyly.

'No honour—how could I forget you? I believe that

I did not then meet your companion—for I would have remembered her, too.'

Athene, noting that Nick was glowering at her—as usual—found herself liking this blunt young man. 'No, Angmering,' she offered, 'I was not present because my mama was ill, and so we were unable to attend.'

'You reside in Abbot Quincey, Miss Filmer?'

Athene shook her head. 'No, I live with my mother, who is a widow, in a hamlet called Steep Ride at the other end of Steepwood. It is very pretty—perhaps because it is so small.'

Steep Ride, said Nick to himself. I must remember that. I now have the opportunity to find out more about Miss Athene Filmer and her origins. He was on his own. Adrian had Emma on his arm, and Marcus was escorting Athene. He could hear what they were saying and it did not please him.

After a short time during which they engaged in the small change of conversation, Marcus said to her, 'You are the first person, Miss Filmer, to whom I have spoken since I arrived in London who did not look at me as though I were about to do something strange and remarkable. I congratulate you.'

'Oh,' said Athene, smiling, 'I am sure that if you wanted to do something strange and remarkable, you would, but at the moment I do not expect it of you. I suppose that it is the Marquis's murder and your family's association with Steepwood which is causing everyone to behave as though we are all in the middle of a Drury Lane melodrama.'

Marcus smiled at her. 'Well put, Miss Filmer. You have succeeded in making me laugh at what was previously annoying me. Nick Cameron told me that you were a clever young woman, and so you are.'

'Did he, indeed?' said Athene dryly. 'I suppose, seeing that he has a reputation for being clever, that I should be flattered.'

'No flattery—as I am sure that he would agree.'

Athene doubted that very much. She was not sure how much she liked, or trusted, Mr Nicholas Cameron. What she did know was something which annoyed her: that she was, in some mysterious fashion, greatly drawn to him. Whenever she entered a room or, as on this occasion, was driven into Hyde Park, she found herself looking around for him. Worse than that, simply meeting him was strangely exciting: the sensation which he always aroused in her was very similar to the one occasion when she had, by accident, taken too much strong drink.

How stupid to say that the mere sight of a man could make her light-headed! It made her wonder what effect she had on *him*. She usually gained the impression that she annoyed him: his mouth always thinned at the sight of her, and the eyes which surveyed her were so coldly assessing.

Nick, just behind them, was in nearly as great an emotional turmoil as Athene. He was having the same thoughts about her as she was about him. He could not help overhearing her conversation with Angmering and, as a consequence, was more determined than ever to find as much out about her as he could.

His determination was reinforced when the Duke of Inglesham, whose carriage was parked beneath some trees, came walking over to them, accompanied by a large borzoi which he was leading on a silver chain.

On reaching Athene the borzoi was immediately as enraptured by her as most male animals appeared to be, and had to be restrained by his master from embracing her.

Inglesham said in his usual cool fashion, 'Angmering, my friend, you must introduce me to your charming companion so that I may apologise to her for the conduct of my animal, whom I have rightly named Ivan the Terrible, although he is not usually quite so mischievous.'

He bowed low to Athene when he had finished.

Another damned admirer, was Nick's furious thought. She ought to be named Aphrodite, goddess of love, not Athene, since every man appears to be ready to fall at her feet. She would not lack for customers if she set herself up as a courtesan, that's for sure!

Marcus was busy introducing Athene to the Duke—and to Ivan, who was barking his approval at her. She bent down to stroke his proud and haughty head, which simply resulted in her being rewarded with enthusiastic lickings of her hand.

The Duke, pulling Ivan away, overwhelmed her with apologies, ending with, 'My dear Miss Filmer, I can only say that I have never known him to behave in such an extreme fashion before. He has previously been distinguished by his dislike of human beings—and that includes myself. You should count yourself flattered.'

Flattery again! Athene smiled and Nick ground his teeth—which was something of a feat, since he was trying to look pleased at the Duke's advent and his conversation with them. Inglesham's reputation was that of a hermit, and he usually had little to do with his fellow men and women. It was rumoured that he had been disappointed in love in his youth, that his marriage had been desperately unhappy, and that since his wife's death he had become more of a re-cluse than ever.

And now here he was, making eyes at Miss Athene Filmer, and his damned dog had nothing better to do than imitate his master. It was at this point in his internal rantings that Nick Cameron realised that something appalling had happened: he was in love with Miss Athene Filmer himself, and every male animal, human or beast, was his rival!

No, it was not to be borne, it was lust he must be experiencing. Yes, that was it, lust; but he knew that it was a lie. He might deceive others, including Athene; but he could not deceive himself.

There was no doubt that the Duke was struck by her.

'Athene,' he was saying. 'A noble name: may I enquire whether it is a family one?'

'I don't think so,' said Athene, whose only family was her mother, but she could not tell the Duke so. 'My mother called me that because her father had been a great classicist and she thought the name a pretty one.'

'No prettier than its possessor,' said the Duke gallantly, again trying to restrain Ivan, who had for some minutes been gazing adoringly at her, but was now ready to lick her again. 'I understand from what Angmering has just said that you are in London as the friend of a daughter of the Tenison family who hail from Steepwood in Northants. I believe I met Tenison recently over some wretched business with the late Marquis of Sywell.'

'Possibly,' said Athene, trying to give away as little of her unhappy origins as possible. 'I know that he was engaged in some trouble over disputed boundaries.'

'Were you here on your own account I would have made you a present of Ivan, who, I fear, will be distraught when he is compelled to leave you. You, I take it, come from Steepwood, as well. You have relatives there? Your mama's, perhaps.'

Now what the devil is he at? thought both Marcus and Nick. They were each privately of the opinion that he was attracted to Miss Athene Filmer, which was a monstrously odd supposition, knowing the Duke's reputation for rectitude in all aspects of his life.

'None that I am aware of,' said Athene, who was beginning to feel a great deal of embarrassment as the Duke pursued the question of her family. Although she showed little outward sign of this, Nick's sensitivity to her every mood told him that the Duke was treading on thorny ground. What was even more interesting was that the Duke was doing it at all.

What the devil did he want with Athene?

Athene was asking herself the same question. She was absently patting Ivan's head, for that animal was now content to enjoy her mere company without being over-enthusiastic about it. She was thinking that if she had been anyone but the Tenisons' poor friend she would have gladly accepted the present of the dog. She had never possessed one. Mrs Filmer had always lived on the edge of poverty: her annuity was enough to keep her in only modest comfort, so the Filmer women had always kept a cat which was less expensive than a dog.

'Like the old witches of legend,' Athene's mother had once said with a sigh.

The Duke, sensing that he was going a little too far and too fast, rapidly and tactfully abandoned Athene and her family to speak generally of the recent Luddite murder of a merchant in Yorkshire and the sad state of the lower classes in England.

'It is the war,' he said, with Nick and Marcus nodding agreement. 'Things might have been bad enough without that and the French blockade, which has only made matters worse. Young Byron was right to raise the matter in the Lords, but while he expressed his indignation, he failed to suggest any practical measures which might alleviate suffering.'

Well, at least he's no longer badgering me about my non-existent relatives, thought Athene, but this is nearly as melancholy a subject. It came almost as a relief when Adrian, Emma on his arm, returned to greet them with, 'What the deuce happened to you and Angmering, Nick, that you fell behind...'

He was interrupted by Ivan, who had taken an instant dislike to him and had begun to bark furiously at him.

The Duke said, 'Bad dog. I must return you to the carriage. I'm sorry to leave so cavalierly, Kinloch, but I really must not allow Ivan to dominate the conversation. We may speak again another time. Delighted to meet you all, and to be introduced to you, Miss Filmer: honoured I am sure.' He bowed himself away, dragging after him an angry Ivan.

'Now, what was all that about?' exclaimed Adrian, staring after him. 'Was he the reason that you fell behind? Thought the man was supposed to be a hermit. Didn't care for the way he looked at you, Athene, nor his dog, either.'

The rest of the party refrained from laughing at his artless comment. There were times when Adrian in spite of, or perhaps because of, his simple-mindedness, came out with the very truths which the more subtle-minded suppressed, and this was one of them.

Athene remarked in as cool a voice as she could summon up, 'I think, Adrian, that he only paid attention to me because of the extraordinary behaviour of his dog.'

She was not being strictly truthful. There had been something insistent in the Duke's questioning of her, and whether this was because she had attracted him, or whether he had genuinely wished to learn of her family, she was not sure. Again, all unknowingly, her thoughts were an echo of Nick's.

Marcus, too, had been intrigued by the Duke's behaviour to Athene but before he could say anything, which he thought later was just as well, their party was accosted by an extremely well-dressed and handsome woman who appeared to be in her early thirties and was on the arm of an elderly man.

'Cameron! Nick Cameron, it *is* you. I thought it was, but Laxford wasn't sure. His sight's not what it was these days. How extremely delightful to meet you again, after so many years. You must know,' she announced addressing all her hearers as though she were running a public meeting, 'that Nick and I were playmates when we were children. Ah, happy days,' she sighed, and then, briskly, 'Pray introduce me to your new friends, Nick. Lord Kinloch and I are old ones.'

And all the time the elderly man, her husband, Lord Laxford, stood mumchance beside her.

Athene noticed that Nick, far from looking delighted by Lady Laxford's effusive greeting, had assumed the expression which he always wore when he was busily engaged in chiding her.

His bow to the lady was perfunctory, and he did not address her by her title, saying only, 'Very well, Flora, it shall be as you wish.'

More than that his manner was icy as, one by one, he made the demanded introductions to a lady whose beautiful face was marred by a pair of shrewd, assessing eyes. What interested Athene was that the person the eyes were assessing was none other than herself. So Nick's playmate was clever enough—or knew him well enough—to be aware that it was she who was the object of his interest and not Emma!

Now what did that tell her about the lady—and her relationship with Nick?

Small talk followed in which Nick played no part, even when Lady Laxford dragged him into the conversation with, 'Silent, Nick, most unlike you.'

He preferred instead to stand to one side and try to engage the interest of the Lady's Lord, whose baffled gaze indicated that old age had somewhat addled his wits. Despite this obvious fact his much younger wife frequently appealed to him most prettily, but never waited for the answer which she knew that she was never going to get.

Finally, to everyone's relief, Flora Laxford's husband tugged at her arm and muttered something in a hoarse, incomprehensible voice to which she responded with a little shriek, and, 'Oh, very well, my dear. We'll return to the carriage where you may make yourself comfortable. I'll bid *au revoir* to my new and old friends.'

With a nod of the head and a wave of the hand she moved away, dragging along her better-half, who might, thought Nick morosely, be more accurately described as her worst-half.

Everyone looked at everyone else, not knowing quite what to say. Marcus, indeed, in his usual bluff fashion, was the only one to come out with the socially unsayable. 'Goodness me, what an exhausting creature. Were you really bosom bows with her in your distant childhood, Cameron?'

'For a time,' he replied in a voice which was designed to deter further confidences.

To see Flora Campbell again, and so suddenly, had been a shock to him. Oh, she was still pretty, but had she always been so shallow? He tried to push the unhappy memories which her reappearance had revived to what he thought of as the dustbin of his mind, but found it difficult.

Fortunately for him, a distant cousin of Marcus's arrived who wished him to join his party on the other side of the park in order to assure the cousin's mama that neither Marcus nor his father were in danger of immediate arrest over Sywell's murder.

This meant that Adrian was now able to escort Athene and Nick took over Emma. He found her pleasant, but undemanding, and as unlike Athene as a girl could be.

She told him, quite artlessly, 'I was so relieved when Mama asked Athene to accompany us to London. She looked after me at school, you know, when I first went there. Some of the girls began to bully me because I was young and small, but she soon made short work of them. I owe her a great deal which I can never really repay.'

These acts of kindness described an Athene whom Nick did not know. On the other hand, he thought cynically, it was quite possible that she had cultivated Emma in order to secure her parents' patronage.

The more he learned of her the more determined he became to learn even more. Not only that, meeting Flora Campbell again had revived all his suspicion of women and their motives. He could never forget that they had once been friends, and later more than friends. They had laughed, walked and played together and he had thought himself secure in his love for her. Before he had left for his last term at university, he had proposed to her and arrangements had begun so that they might be married as soon as he returned home.

The marriage had not taken place. While he was away she had met Lord Laxford, already an old man who was looking for a young wife. Laxford was immensely rich, with a fortune nearly as great as Adrian's, so instead of marrying the girl he loved, and whom he thought had loved him, Nick had been condemned to hear of her grand wedding to another.

Worse was yet to come. On the first occasion on which they met again, some six months later, he had sought to reproach her for her faithlessness, and she had laughed at him.

The woman he had thought so pure and true had said, 'Oh, Nick, my darling, don't be stupid. Nothing has changed, we can have one another whenever we wish and when Laxford goes to his last rest, which cannot be long, I shall be left with a dowry which will make us rich and comfortable when we marry, instead of merely being content to trudge along on just enough.'

He had turned away from her in disgust, all his youthful ideals destroyed in an instant. She had made him hard and cynical, not only towards women, but towards humanity in general. He did not, could not, regret having lost her, for she was not worth having, but what she had done had changed him completely. Later, when Laxford took a long time in dying, she had tried to approach him again, but he had always refused her.

Only when she had cornered him in the company of friends, as she had just done, was he unable to hold her off as he might have liked, but the inevitable result of her having done so was that he hardened himself further against Athene.

Tomorrow he would contact his cousin Hugh Cameron, who worked in the Home Office, and ask him to recommend an ex-Bow Street Runner whom he could send to Steepwood to find out exactly who and what Miss Athene Filmer actually was.

And in the doing he might discover something that would set his mind at rest where this charming mermaid was concerned.

Or not—as the case might be!

CHAPTER FIVE

Cousin Hugh Cameron duly obliged. He had a soft spot for Nick, particularly since his other cousin, Jack, a Captain in the 73rd Highland Regiment, was a black sheep with whom he felt no affinity. 'Jackson's your man,' he said. 'He's damnably discreet and, to let you into a secret, he left the Runners because we like to use him unofficially. At the moment he's free. I won't ask you why you need him. As he's fond of saying, mum's the word in these matters.'

'You're a good fellow. Tell me where to find him.'

'Oh, and by the way,' Hugh said when he had duly done so, 'you'll be pleased to learn that Cousin Jack has been sent to the Antipodes to guard convicts in Botany Bay, so he won't be writing you any more begging letters for some time yet!'

Jackson turned out to look exactly as Nick had expected. He was a dour, stocky, but powerful man, who never questioned Nick as to why he wanted to discover everything there was to be known about Miss Athene Filmer and her family.

He simply nodded his head, before saying in his rough voice, 'You will be aware, sir, that what I may find out might not be to your liking. I always warn folk of that, since sometimes they reproach me bitterly over any bad news which I might bring them. After all, I am only its messenger, not the creator of it.'

'Good, or bad, I wish to know everything which you might unearth,' Nick told him. 'And I certainly shan't blame you if it proves to be bad.'

Jackson nodded. 'Fair enough. I like to know where I stand.'

He did not ask, 'Pretty young lady, is she?' because he didn't think that Mr Nicholas Cameron would be troubling his clever head over an ugly one. What was more, he didn't tell Mr Cameron that other parties were interested in the goings-on at Steepwood in Northants: it was none of his business.

It was his, Jackson's, though, and besides foraging around about the Marquis of Sywell's untimely end, he had yet a third, if minor, errand to carry out. The devil of it was that this meant that he would have to be more discreet than usual—the good thing was that he would make more money than his usual commissions guaranteed him because he would have only one lot of travelling expenses.

Emma was duly presented to the Prince Regent, who turned out to be a dreadful disappointment.

'He was a fat old man,' she told Athene despondently. 'And very ugly. Papa said that he had been handsome in youth but that he has gone to seed badly. A very fat old woman was pointed out to me as his lady friend. It seems that he likes them ugly.'

Yes, decidedly Emma was growing up. That same night the Tenisons gave a little reception to which only their intimate friends were invited. Poor Athene was made to resume her homely grey dress again, since Mrs Tenison had begun to realise that she was outshining Emma—nor was she allowed to sit down to dinner with the most favoured guests before the reception began.

Not that it made any difference to her admirers. Adrian, indeed, would have complained loudly about her absence, but Nick persuaded him that it would not be tactful.

'Worse than that,' he said, 'it might provoke the old dragon into dismissing her, which would mean that you would lose the opportunity to meet her again.'

'There is that,' Adrian agreed, and the moment that Athene appeared in the main drawing-room after dinner was over he immediately made a bee-line for her, his honest face glowing with indignation.

'So old mother Tenison banned you from the dinner party,' he said. 'I wanted to give her a piece of my mind, but Nick stopped me.'

'Quite right, too,' she told him, a little surprised that Nick should protect her from what would inevitably have been Emma's mother's wrath. 'I think that she is beginning to regret that she brought me to London, and I fear that your intervention might give her the opportunity to get rid of me.'

She spoke more truly than she knew. Mrs Tenison had already told her husband that she was of a mind to send Filmer back to Northamptonshire.

'That would be a great mistake, my dear,' he said gently. 'Emma is beginning to blossom, and a great deal of her improvement is due to Miss Filmer, who seems to know how to persuade her to overcome her lack of confidence.'

'But Filmer has set her sights on young Kinloch,' said his wife angrily, 'and I was hoping that he would show an interest in Emma. He will not do that while he is besotted with her companion. Not that Filmer behaves like one.'

'I agree,' he said, 'most companions suppress their charges. Miss Filmer, on the other hand, brings Emma out. As for Kinloch, you must leave him to make up his own mind. He is not, for all his simplicity, easily influenced. Besides, I have a feeling that matters at the moment are in a state of flux. Kinloch undoubtedly admires Miss Filmer, but remember, there are two parties to consider here.'

'If by that,' said Mrs Tenison inelegantly, 'you mean that when she gets the chance Filmer will not hook him and lead him to the altar, then I believe that you are gravely mistaken.'

'It is no mistake of mine,' he said gently, 'that Miss

Filmer is a clever young woman and Lord Kinloch, whatever his other virtues, is exceedingly backward in that line. Well, we shall see, but I think that you worry unnecessarily.'

Mr Tenison did not believe it would be wise to explain to his wife exactly why he was uncertain that Athene and Lord Kinloch would arrive at the altar because he did not think that her mind was subtle enough to understand what he saw as the undercurrents of their relationship. She was blind to all the hints and clues which her quiet husband was picking up, and saw Nick Cameron as only a none too wealthy hanger-on of his cousin.

On top of that, Nick's cleverness was beyond her. She did not value it, nor recognise it when she saw it in Athene and in her own husband. Her judgement of men and women was essentially superficial, and Mr Tenison feared that if she were not careful her obvious manoeuvrings in search of a husband for her daughter would ultimately be to Emma's detriment.

In the meantime Adrian danced attendance on Athene and included Emma in their orbit because that was the only way in which he could pursue the real object of his desire. Emma, indeed, was so innocent that the possibilities which troubled her mother never entered her head.

She liked Adrian, and when he started a jolly game of whist in an anteroom after he had persuaded Marcus Angmering to partner Emma while he partnered Athene, she was over the moon with delight.

The game was jolly because the players were not very serious, and Nick Cameron, a sardonic onlooker, was amused to discover how each of them betrayed their character in the manner in which they played their cards.

Marcus was all bluff aggression: he invariably overplayed his hand. Emma by contrast was prudent, but the nuances of the game were beyond her. Adrian played like the happy artless boy he was, while Athene showed an appreciation of the game's possibilities which was beyond that of the other contestants.

The sad joke of it was that, saddled with Adrian, she was invariably on the losing side. Nick suspected that were she his partner they could have taken on any pair whom the guests at the reception could have provided. The game ran out with a delighted Emma and her partner as easy winners. Emma's pleasure was all the greater because she had always previously been on the losing side.

'Now, Kinloch,' said Marcus, 'you must, as a penance for losing, pay for us all to go to Astley's amphitheatre as soon as you can book seats. The ladies have informed me that they have never gone there, and it is time that they did.'

'Pleased to oblige,' grinned Adrian, telling himself that it would be a splendid opportunity for him to hold Athene's hand in the dark of the box—why, he might even snatch a kiss. 'Nick should come, too, though.'

'If I must,' Nick said. He was trying not to sound

ungracious, but for some reason the thought of Athene and Adrian being together was beginning to disturb him mightily.

'Who taught you to play as well as that?' he asked her when, the game over, she walked away, telling herself that with Mrs Tenison's stern eye on her she must not monopolise Adrian too much.

'Mr Tenison,' she said, 'and the local vicar when they needed another lady, and since Emma has no real talent for the game, and her father found that I had, I was included in their foursome. Mrs Tenison was the vicar's partner.'

The small beer of country life, thought Nick, and Pallas Athene is a quick learner, no doubt of that.

'I should not like to play against you for money,' he told her, half seriously.

'No?' she raised her eyebrows at him. 'I think that you do not like to have much to do with me, sir, whether money is involved or not.'

She had inadvertently offered him a chance to throw a dart at her.

'Oh, Pallas Athene, I think that money has a great deal to do with why Adrian and I meet you so often, and I do not think that it is my money in which you are interested.'

Athene was surprised at how much this judgement, carelessly thrown in her direction, hurt her. That there was some measure of truth in it made the hurt greater.

'You are not kind, sir,' she told him, her beautiful mouth quivering a little. 'You will allow me to leave you, after informing you that I have never once thought of money either when with you, or away from you.'

Was that a tear gathering in her eye? He had not meant to touch her to the quick, but he had. He had thought her harder than she was: always before she had turned his poisoned arrows aside easily. Why had this time been different?

Nick found himself beginning to apologise.

'Athene,' he said, 'forgive me. That statement was unwarrantable. I had no right to make it. But...'

'Oh, there is always a but attached to whatever you are about to say,' she told him hardily, quite recovered from her moment of fleeting distress. 'Pray spare me the rest of the sentence. I am sure you were merely about to reproach me after a different fashion.'

If only she were as virtuous as she was witty and clever, what a nonpareil she would be: all the same, she had made him feel like a cur.

Nick opened his mouth. He was too late. Not only was there nothing which he could usefully say, but she was now so far away that to pursue her, mouthing apologies, would undoubtedly cause unkind comment.

All that he had done was to throw her into his cousin's arms, for Adrian had come looking for her. He was saying tenderly, 'My pretty dear, you look tired. Shall we find somewhere quiet to sit, away from the hurly burly?' and she was agreeing with him and they were out of Nick's line of sight.

Nick stopped cursing himself and began to hope that Jackson might bring him some news which would show the woman with whom he had inconveniently fallen in love in a better light.

Jackson was already installed in Abbot Quincey's cheapest inn. He had arrived in Northampton the previous day, and had hired a horse to take him deep into Steepwood. The landlord was a gossip and his talk was all about the dead Marquis and his runaway wife. There had been no need for him to raise the subject.

'Only mystery about that devil's end,' the landlord told him cheerfully, 'was why nobody ever did for him before. The one thing that can be said in his favour was that the gossip about him kept us all entertained for years.'

'Plenty of gossip still,' Jackson had said idly, hiding his face in a foaming pint of indifferent ale.

'Aye, mind you, I don't think that Lord Yardley did for him. The Earl's a real gent. Sywell's wife, now, that's another matter. He was a cruel beast there, and no mistake. Gave her a black eye more'n once. No way to treat a lady.'

'Or someone who wasn't a lady, either,' was Jackson's dry contribution. 'Who d'you think *did* do for him, then?'

'Hard to say. But the way he was done for wasn't a lady's way—though she might have paid for someone to do him for her, if she's still alive, that is. There are those who believe that he did for her—only her body has never turned up, so if he did kill her, he couldn't have been tried without a body. Too late, now, if one does turn up.'

'Wouldn't prove he'd done it,' offered Jackson.

'Aye, there is that. Another pint?'

'Wouldn't mind,' said Jackson, hoping that finding information about Miss Athene Filmer wasn't going to be as difficult as discovering something substantial about Sywell's murder and his wife's disappearance. Hugh Cameron had hinted that the Regent himself wished the murderer to be found as soon as possible. It seemed that he thought that yet another unsolved scandal in high life would be one too many.

Jackson didn't care how many scandals there were so long as he was paid for investigating them. One thing was odd about his present commissions: that the subjects of both of the major ones were, or had been, inhabitants of this wild and, up to the present, little-known corner of Northamptonshire. Since he didn't believe in coincidences, he wondered what the connection was between the Marquis of Sywell, his wife and Miss Athene Filmer and whether he could uncover it. The minor commission also involved the Steepwood district, but he didn't think that there were any hidden connections there with the other two.

He stopped showing any further interest in Sywell lest the landlord began to wonder why he, a stranger, was so interested in him, but his lack of interest lost him nothing, since everyone who visited the inn had only one subject of conversation and that was the late Marquis. Jackson only had to sit there, apparently half-asleep and listen to the buzzing going on around him, to gather even more information than if he had been busy questioning everyone.

One piece of gossip which he overheard while apparently half-dozing intrigued him. The name of Tenison was bandied about the bar as proof that the Marquis could rile even the mildest of men.

'Arguing about boundary lines between Abbey land and Tenison's, weren't they, and Tenison swore that he'd set the law on him if he didn't give way. Story was that the mad Marquis kept on shouting that it was a pity they weren't living in the old days, when he would have had Tenison hanged for his insolence to such a magnate as he was. Parson said as how he'd never seen Tenison so angry before.'

'Angry enough to do for him?'

'Perhaps, who knows?'

So Miss Filmer's employer was another who had fallen foul of the madman, and that would give him a fine excuse to visit Tenison and while questioning him weigh up Athene Filmer.

Dawn the next day saw the sun rising in a blue sky. A good time to saddle up and visit all the oddly named villages which were distributed around the old Abbey. While he was doing that he could think up some convincing reason for visiting the Abbey itself when he had finished investigating Miss Filmer.

Abbot Giles was his first destination. He rode down

the main street looking about him as though he were trying to find something. An old lady carrying a basket and with an equally elderly dog on a long lead seemed to be the kind of person who might know all the local gossip. He was well aware that the Filmers and the Tenisons lived at Steep Ride, but he was prepared to believe that in this odd corner of the world everyone knew everyone else. Besides, he'd always found that an indirect approach paid off.

He dismounted, hitched his horse to a nearby gatepost and walked towards the old girl, pulling off his battered hat.

'Excuse me, madam, but I wonder whether you could assist me? I seem to have been given an incorrect address. I was told to visit Datchet House in the main street here where the party I seek lives, but there seems to be no such place.'

A pair of sharp eyes scrutinised him with interest.

'Indeed there is not. You must have been misinformed. What, may I ask, is the name of your party?'

'A Miss Athene Filmer. I have a letter to deliver to her.'

'Oh, Miss Filmer! Yes, she did live at Datchet House, but that is situated in Steep Ride—I can give you some useful directions. You will not find Miss Filmer there, though, only her mother. Miss Filmer is in London. She has gone as a companion for the Tenisons' young daughter.'

The sharp eyes on him were curious and avid for information.

'You seem a knowledgeable lady, madam. I wonder whether you can help me further. I also have a patron who is anxious to discover the whereabouts of the Marchioness of Sywell—that is, if she is still alive. Have you any notion where she might have gone to?'

'How curious you should ask me *that*. I have none at all, but the young woman whom you seek might. I happen to know that she and Louise Sywell were very friendly. I found that out by the purest accident. My walks take me into the Abbey grounds and on several occasions I saw them walking and talking together. Quite by chance I saw the Marchioness there on the day before she disappeared. She was not with Miss Filmer, but was in the Sacred Grove, by the Rune Stone. I gained the impression that she had been weeping.'

So the Marchioness and Nick Cameron's lady had been bosom bows. Here was a right royal turn-up!

He was about to ask another question when the old lady said to him eagerly, only too delighted to have a new ear to pour her gossip into, 'I was not at all surprised that Miss Filmer and the Marchioness were friends. They were both of quite mysterious origin. Miss Filmer's mother calls herself a widow but I have my doubts about that. She came here when Athene was a baby and never a relative has visited her. Oh, she seems respectable enough, but one must admit that her situation is extremely odd. Is there or was there a Mr Filmer? One begs leave to doubt it. Not that Miss Filmer is other than a well-behaved young woman, you understand. Quite clever, they say, but one cannot hold that against her. Is there anything further I can help you with?'

'It would be useful if you could let me have the London address of Miss Filmer's employer so that I can arrange for a letter to be delivered there. I am exceedingly grateful to you for your assistance, madam,' Jackson said. He was being completely truthful. 'May I know your name so that I may write you a formal letter of thanks?'

'Indeed, you may. I am Miss Amy Rushmere and I live at the end house in the street in that direction. If you will come with me, I shall write down the Tenisons' address, and perhaps you would welcome a dish of tea while I do so.'

Jackson heartily agreed to drink tea with her, for the old gossip had saved him a deal of work. Had she told the authorities of the Marchioness's friendship with Miss Filmer? He would seek that young lady out when he returned to London and question her about it. The Marchioness might have said something to her which meant little at the time, but which his gentle prodding of her memory might bring to her mind. It was also quite possible that the Marchioness had confided in her before she disappeared.

Miss Rushmere had little further to tell him, but questioned him eagerly about London, after she had given him the Tenisons' address, which he already knew.

'I only visited London once,' she told him, 'when I was a girl. I understand it is greatly changed.'

He told her it was, before setting out on his travels again. He thought that a visit to Steep Ride might be useful. He found, however, little there to engage him. Datchet House was small and it was plain that its owner did not possess a great deal of tin, but neither was she poverty-stricken. Since Mrs Filmer appeared to have no occupation it must be assumed that she had some sort of income: an annuity perhaps? He had no intention of rousing further unnecessary speculation by visiting her. He thought that the old gossip had told him everything he needed to know about her and her daughter, and since Mrs Filmer had kept the secret of the identity of her unknown lover for over twenty years she was scarcely likely to blab it to him at first sight.

He had already discovered that the only bank hereabouts was a country one in Abbot Quincey, which contained the few shops and the small Assembly Rooms, which were actually a ballroom over the Angel inn, which made up the social life and the provender of gossip in the Steepwood district. He would go there, find out if there was a clerk whom he could bribe for information—and bribe him.

In the meantime he would continue his investigations into the matter of Sywell's death and his lady's disappearance.

* * *

Bribing the clerk was easier than Jackson had thought it might be. He visited Jordan's Bank, looked about him, and identified one scrawny-looking, threadbare underling occupying the bank's only public counter. He wore a permanently dissatisfied face.

Jackson presented a Treasury note for five pounds and asked to be given five sovereigns.

'Don't see many of these,' sighed the clerk, holding up the note before sliding the sovereigns across.

'Nor many sovereigns, either,' said Jackson who had rapidly summed up his man.

'You can say that again, sir. Pays badly, does Banker Jordan.'

'You might like to earn a little extra tin, perhaps,' offered Jackson, playing the Devil to the clerk's Doctor Faustus.

'Why, are you giving sovereigns away?'

'Come to the alehouse tonight, answer a few questions and I'll give you a half-sovereign for each of them—provided that you say nothing of this to anyone.'

'Take me for a fool, do you? I'll be there on the stroke of seven, and you'd better be there, too.'

Oh, yes, Jackson would be there, no doubt of it. Beneath the battered clock on the greasy wall, seated beside the fire, a pot of ale before him. He had no doubt that the clerk would be there, too—and so he was.

'Fire away, old fellow,' the clerk said eagerly, already spending the half-sovereigns.

'Over here,' said Jackson, moving into a pew set

away from the rest of the room, ensuring privacy for its occupants, after ordering a pot of ale for the clerk.

'I am assuming that the bank has a Mrs Charlotte Filmer for a customer.'

'Indeed, sir, indeed. Is that your first question?'

'Yes.' Jackson laid a sovereign on the table. 'Now earn the rest of it. Do I also assume that she has an income, probably paid into the bank quarterly?'

'Yes, she does,' grinned the clerk. This was easy. He was supposed to keep all customers' business confidential, but damn that for a tale if sovereigns were on offer.

'Now earn another sovereign by answering two questions. Is it in the form of a banker's draft, and if so on what bank?'

Oh, this was easy money indeed, for he knew the answers to his new friend's questions.

'A draft for a hundred pounds paid quarterly. It is drawn on Coutts.'

'Excellent, now let us drink our ale in the knowledge of work well done.'

Jackson slid the two sovereigns across the table, and the two of them drank to each other before Jackson leaned forward and said with quiet savagery, 'And if you tell anyone of this, I'll have your guts for garters, make no mistake.'

'Oh, mum's the word, sir, mum's the word,' chattered the clerk. 'By my life, sir. You may depend on me.'

'Good, I'd hate for you to have a nasty accident.

Enjoy your windfall and forget that you ever met me. And, one last thing, don't visit this alehouse until after I leave the district at the week's end.'

Jackson leaned back and enjoyed his ale. So, Miss Athene Filmer was someone's love child, and her mother was being paid off by a draft drawn on Coutts. By whom, he would never discover through Coutts, for the bank's confidentiality was rarely, if ever, breached. One thing was sure, though, anyone who banked with Coutts had both position and money— which told him something about the donor.

As a bonus Miss Filmer was Louise Sywell's friend—and there was another lead for him to follow, and another fact for Mr Nicholas Cameron.

It also meant that before he reported back to all his employers he would need to interview the interesting and clever Miss Filmer, whose name seemed to pop up at every turn.

Some feeling, some intuition which he never ignored when he was in the middle of an investigation such as this, told him that Miss Filmer might be the one person who could lead him to the missing Marchioness. He had no concrete evidence to support this belief, but no matter. When he visited the Tenisons in London he would take the opportunity to question her about her friendship with the missing Marchioness, citing his commission from the Home Office as giving him the right to do so. Naturally, he would say nothing to her which would give away his commission from Nick Cameron regarding her origins and reputation!

His final task was to gain entry to the Abbey itself, which he duly did by the simple expedient of breaking into it one night. He found nothing there of the slightest use to him. The bedroom where Sywell had been murdered had been cleaned up after a fashion, and his own easy illegal entry, made while Burneck was out drinking, told him that the murderer's entry had probably been equally as easy. Burneck he met, by apparent accident, in the Angel's taproom, but he gained nothing by talking to him. 'I was absent that night,' he offered, 'fortunately for me. I was over at Jaffrey House, as a dozen could tell you,' and nothing could shake him.

Jackson thought that confined to a cell in Newgate, where he could be manhandled at leisure, he might sing a different song, but there was no scrap of evidence which could justify detaining him, so that was that. Best to return to London and seek out the interesting Miss Filmer under the guise of questioning the Tenisons.

Dammit, thought Nick Cameron, more in resignation than in anger, what the devil is the man up to? He was watching the Duke of Inglesham make his way to their party, who were chatting together after having enjoyed the performance of a Haydn quartet at one of Lady Dunlop's musical soirées.

The reclusive Duke, who for years had never been

seen anywhere, was now being seen everywhere. And in that everywhere he always chose—apparently absent-mindedly—to pay his respects to the Tenisons before he had been in the room with them for five minutes!

Like Mr Tenison the Duke was bookish, and after he had done the pretty with all the Tenison party, he invariably began to converse with him at length upon all the erudite subjects which engaged both their interests. This was perhaps reasonable enough and could be considered as perfectly normal behaviour for two middle-aged men, except that the Duke always took the trouble to include Athene in their discussions, which today had centred around an appreciation of what they had just heard.

Oh, she never disgraced herself when he did: she was, being very well-read, perfectly able to join them in their wordplay whilst Adrian, not understanding anything which was being said, was happy to stand back—open-mouthed—admiring his beloved's wit and charm.

Nick, more worldly-wise, was asking himself whether it was Mr Tenison's scholarship which attracted the Duke—or was he merely a blind behind which the Duke was able to admire Athene and constantly encourage her to speak her mind?

Not that she needed much encouragement to do *that,* he thought a trifle glumly, having felt the edge of her tongue more than once.

Their conversation, which now included a somewhat baffled Mrs Tenison and Emma, who had just returned from the supper room, had moved on to a learned discussion on the origin of the place names around Steepwood Abbey.

'Steep Ride,' mused the Duke after Mr Tenison had told him that his family came from that village. 'I suppose it must either refer to the River Steep or to a small wooded hill there with a track, suitable for horsemen to ride up or down.'

'A very small one,' admitted Mr Tenison.

'And you, Miss Athene,' asked the Duke turning his penetrating eyes on her, 'do you come from Steep Ride? I can imagine that on long winter nights your father and Mr Tenison must have had some interesting chats about its name.'

'Alas, Duke,' said Athene, who was as puzzled as Nick by the Duke's interest in her, 'my father is long dead. I live with my mother, who has never remarried.'

A shadow passed across the Duke's face. He expressed his condolences before droning away—Adrian's words—about place names again and how those in the Midlands differed from those in the north and the south.

Ordinarily Nick would have enjoyed taking part in such a discussion, but his reservations and doubts about the Duke's behaviour prevented him from doing so. The thought that Inglesham might be using his erudition as a blind behind which to pursue Athene was quite spoiling his evening.

It was bad enough to have to endure Adrian, his friend and cousin, sniffing around her, but to watch a middle-aged Duke doing the same was even worse. Even the Duke's departure shortly afterwards did not sweeten his temper.

He took advantage of another pause in the programme, designed to allow the guests a further visit to the supper room, to take Athene by the arm and say, between gritted teeth, 'All that learned piff-paff must have exhausted you, my dear Pallas. Allow me to refresh your spirits by leading you to where I understand from Mrs Tenison there is an excellent display of food and drink. Unless of course, like your namesake, you prefer to partake of the food of the gods—whatever that might be.'

This was too bad of him, was it not? For was not his behaviour a form of blackmail, so that there was nothing for it but to allow him to walk her to where footmen paraded with wine and meat and salmon patties on trays, and where a buffet of unparalleled splendour and dimensions was laid out?

Unfortunately Athene had never felt less like food.

Why did it distress her so much that he disliked her? Why *did* he dislike her? She had done nothing to hurt him. That his cousin—and now the Duke—chose to admire her was not her fault. She had not missed the sour glances which he had thrown her way during the Duke's time with Mr Tenison, but she could not tell him that she was puzzled by the Duke's obvious interest in her, and wished most heartily that he would not single her out so often.

Instead she said, 'What I don't understand, Mr Cameron, is why *you* should so constantly demand to speak to me when you dislike me so much. If being with me makes you so cross, why do you persist in following me about when I obviously find your attentions unwelcome? Unless it is to keep me away from Adrian.'

There was enough truth in her last statement to have him, unwillingly, admire the acuteness of her mind all over again.

'Come now,' he told her, 'can you not believe that I am yet another of your admirers? What is remarkable about that? You have so many that not to admire you has become unfashionable.'

Now *he* was surely telling the truth only in his last statement, for Athene could not believe that he was genuine in saying that he admired her. Oh, if only it were possible that he did. Whenever he was not at odds with her he was a charming companion: he could speak well on matters which interested her, but which were a closed book to his cousin. She had played chess with him at the Tenisons and again when they had all visited Adrian's splendid family home off the Strand, and had given him a good game. Chess was beyond Adrian's understanding.

Nick had found her one day in Adrian's neglected library, admiring the prints which adorned a wall above a set of low bookcases. She had recently asked

Adrian where they had come from and what they sig-
nified, but he had stared blankly at her and had said
dismissively, 'I believe that my grandfather brought
them home from the Grand Tour.'

His lack of interest had been palpable and it had
been left to Nick to enlighten her. 'They are prints by
an Italian master called Piranesi, and they are famous
because they hint at terrible things, but do not show
them happening.'

'Oh, Nick's the clever devil in our family,' Adrian
had once said to her. 'He even paints and draws a
bit.'

Privately she was beginning to wish that she and
Adrian were of a like mind, and that he roused in her
the same sense of excitement which being with Nick
Cameron brought her. Even his dislike of her excited
her and she had made valiant efforts to overcome it:
so far with no success.

'Quiet, tonight, aren't we?' said Nick, seizing a
glass of white wine from a passing tray and offering
it to her.

'I thought that you objected to me being noisy,'
was her riposte to that.

'Only when Inglesham is toadying to you,' Nick
could not prevent himself from saying. 'You know
that he's a great deal richer than Adrian even. Why
don't you pursue *him*? Becoming a Duchess would
crown your Season completely. What's a mere Earl
compared to that?'

Athene lifted her glass defiantly and said, 'I offer

you a toast, Mr Cameron. To your cousin Adrian, who, whatever else he is, is kind. You are not kind. Your cleverness does not attract me as much as his goodness of heart. Does that satisfy you, sir?'

She was shaking so much that the glass in her hand trembled before she lifted it to her mouth; that, and her description of Adrian as kind, shamed him. Also, she had never looked more beautiful, nor sounded more desirable.

Nick had to confess to himself all over again that not only was he madly in love with her despite his suspicion of her motives in encouraging Adrian, but he was equally madly jealous of every man who looked at her, who spoke to her, or on whom she smiled. She would not smile on him. He had been too unkind too often for her to want him. A bitter regret consumed him.

'Athene,' he began, 'I'm sorry…' and was secretly relieved when she stopped him, for he had not known what he might say next.

'No,' she told him, putting her glass down on the table before which they stood. 'I don't want an apology—if that's what you were embarking on. It has come too late. Now, pray excuse me. I do not wish to eat, and I crave for more congenial company.'

Nick made no effort to stop her. She walked away from him straight-backed and only she knew that her heart wept within her, for she was well aware that it was Nick Cameron who could have made her happy, and that Adrian, for her, would always be second-best—despite his kindness.

The Tenisons and Athene were enjoying a late breakfast when the butler announced that a Mr Jackson needed to speak to Mr Tenison and members of his family, on business which was urgent and which pertained to the murder of the Marquis of Sywell. He had the authority of the Home Office to ask questions of parties who might have some useful information to give him.

Jackson had said nothing about the business of the missing Marchioness, since he did not wish Miss Filmer to have time to make up a plausible story if she did have something to hide.

He would spring that on her when he had spoken to Mr Tenison.

'Sywell's death!' exclaimed Mr Tenison, throwing down the *Morning Post* which he had been reading over his coffee and rolls. 'What in the name of wonder does that have to do with me? I was in London when he was murdered. What information could I possibly have which would be of use either to the law or to the Home Secretary?'

'Perhaps our trouble over the boundaries might have come up,' suggested Mrs Tenison, who was not lacking in good sense where such matters were concerned.

'That must be it. Well, I suppose I shall have to

see him. Show him to my study and tell him I will be with him shortly.'

Emma said in a worried voice when her father had left them, 'Surely they cannot imagine that Papa had anything to do with the Marquis's murder?'

Athene put a comforting hand on her arm. 'Dear Emma, the Marquis was killed on the night when we all went to Lady Cowper's ball. Two hundred people must have seen your father there. The man is probably clearing up odds and ends.'

Emma's face cleared, too, and Mrs Tenison grudgingly admitted to herself that Filmer had a deal of common-sense whatever other virtues she lacked. In any case the man did not detain her husband long, for he returned very shortly afterwards to say that he wished to question briefly his wife, Emma and Athene about various matters which he had discovered during a recent visit to Steepwood.

Jackson had no real wish to interview either Mrs Tenison or Emma, but he did not wish to single Athene out. Mr Tenison suggested that he might like to speak to Miss Filmer before he spoke to Emma.

'My daughter is less likely to be over-set if she finds that Miss Filmer returns untroubled from her interview with you. Miss Filmer is a very sensible young woman.'

'Doesn't matter which I see first,' Jackson told him. 'Miss Filmer will do as well as any. Your missis and daughter can come in afterwards.'

Privately he was beginning to be intrigued by Miss

Athene Filmer, who seemed to have made such a great impression on everyone who knew her and whom he had interviewed. She consequently sounded as though she would pay for questioning.

'Question me first?' said Athene doubtfully, and then, echoing Mr Tenison, 'Whatever for?'

'Goodness knows, my dear. He wants to see Mrs Tenison and Emma after you.'

'Oh, very well. But I still find it hard to believe that he really needs to question any of us.'

Athene did not betray it, but her mind was in a turmoil. She was remembering that Louise had warned her that she must not betray her identity as Madame Félice to anyone, and that would even include this emissary from the Government. Mr Tenison had already informed them that Jackson had revealed that he was acting on behalf of the Home Office and—indirectly—of the Regent himself.

Surely, though, the man could not be aware that she knew where the missing Marchioness was and the pseudonym she was currently using? She would have to keep her wits about her and be prepared to lie to him if necessary in order to protect her friend to whom she had promised secrecy.

She found Jackson staring out of the window in Mr Tenison's study, his full attention apparently given to the street below, before the butler's announcing her name had him swinging round to examine her with a pair of yellow eyes which reminded her of the drawing of a lion in one of Mr Tenison's big folios.

'Miss Athene Filmer is it? Pray sit down, my dear. I have a few simple questions to ask you which I am sure that you will be easily able to answer.'

'I hope so, sir,' she told him and gave him her most winning smile.

His answering smile revealed a set of predatory teeth which now had her remembering the Wolf in the fairy story who had bared his to Red Riding Hood, and when she had exclaimed, 'What big teeth you have,' he had replied, 'All the better to eat you with, my dear.'

She knew instinctively that despite his slightly oafish and workmanlike exterior and his blunt speech he was a very clever and dangerous man indeed—something which, unknown to her, Mr Tenison had not quite grasped.

His first questions, though, were innocuous ones which set her wondering why he had needed to interview her at all. They concerned her position in the Tenison household and her address back in Northamptonshire.

'Did you ever meet the Marquis?' Jackson finally asked, after he thought that he had set her completely at ease so that when he introduced the Marchioness into his questioning she would not be afraid of him.

'Not really. I saw him at a distance once. He was thrashing some poor ostler who had done something to distress him, I never knew what. All the girls at Mrs Guarding's school were told to keep well away from him.'

'Um…' He nodded and looked out of the window again as though what he was hearing bored him, and Athene thought hopefully that this interview might rapidly end without any difficult ground having been traversed.

She soon discovered that she was wrong.

In a bored voice he asked, 'And his wife, the Marchioness? She is—or was—a little older than you are. Did you know her?'

Well, at least she could answer that reasonably truthfully.

'A little. When we were small girls she lived at the Abbey and we played together. Then one day, she didn't come to our meeting place, and I never saw her again until the Marquis brought her home after they were married. I didn't recognise her when she was driven by in his carriage, but later on when I was walking in the Abbey grounds, she came up to me and told me that she was my old friend, and after that we met on a few occasions.'

'Um…' said Jackson again. He recognised the ring of truth when he heard it. Yet why was it that he thought that the beautiful young woman opposite to him still had something to tell him? It was not her manner. She was perfectly composed, her elegant hands folded in the lap of her ugly dress.

'Had you seen her recently? Before she disappeared, I mean. Did she give you any notion of where she was going? If she were going anywhere, that is, and has not been done away with.'

Athene could safely tell him the truth about her last meeting with Louise and did. 'I last saw her a few days before her disappearance. She was a good water-colourist and we often met to work and talk together as young women do. We were painting the Rune Stone in the Sacred Grove and she said nothing to indicate that she might be leaving. I did know that she was very unhappy.'

Still the truth. He made as though to speak and she looked levelly at him. Oh, she was a pearl of price was Miss Athene Filmer, for all her illegitimacy. He wondered who the unknown father might be.

He kept silent, apparently thinking, in an effort—a wasted one—to destroy her composure.

'Miss Filmer, I must ask you to be truthful, for it is the government's business I am on, and much hangs on this. Do you have any idea where the Marchioness might be living, or who might be protecting her? A dreadful murder has been committed and she might be implicated. At the least she would repay questioning, and—who knows—it might even exonerate her.'

Now for the lie, and perhaps God would forgive her for not betraying her friend who had been dealt with so harshly by life.

'No, sir, I have no idea. None.'

Athene thought that the less she said the better. Louise had advised her of that, and it was plain that the advice was good.

'None?'

'No, sir.'

'When you had those long walks together did she never speak of any friends elsewhere with whom she might have found shelter?'

Someone at Steepwood had been talking. Who? No matter, she could answer that question truthfully, too. Louise had told her nothing at Steepwood—and so she informed her questioner.

Jackson's admiration for her was unbounded. Beautiful, clever, and the best liar he had ever met. He was sure that she had told him the truth right until he had asked the final question as to whether she knew where Louise Sywell was. How he knew that she was a liar was a mystery to him.

He also knew that he would gain nothing further from her. She was not to be bullied or tricked. The very care with which she had answered him told him that. Her brief answers when he came to the meat of his questioning were masterly.

He decided to try another tack. 'You must, I suppose, Miss Filmer, wish as much as I do that the man who did this dreadful murder is caught before he can commit further atrocities. You must also wish to see your old friend again—if she is still alive that is. I am going to give you an address where you can reach me. If you can think of anything at all which comes to mind and which might help me, then I would be greatly obliged if you would inform me immediately. You would be doing the state some service.'

His last statement baffled Athene. She could not

see what Sywell's murder had to do with the state—
nor poor Louise's whereabouts either.

She had half a mind to question him about that, but
wisely decided that to say as little as possible would
be the best thing. Instead she rose, and said, as coolly
as she could, 'May I go, now?'

'Certainly, Miss Filmer.'

She had her back to him and her hand on the door-
knob when he spoke again. 'You are quite sure that
you have nothing further to tell me, Miss Filmer?'

Athene turned and gave him her most dazzling
smile.

'Quite sure, Mr Jackson.'

CHAPTER SIX

'Questioned you all about Sywell's murder and his wife's disappearance? Whatever for?'

Nick Cameron had just walked over in time to hear Emma telling Adrian about Jackson's visit the previous day and to be amused by hearing Adrian's incredulous response.

The Tenisons, Athene, Nick, Adrian and Marcus Angmering had all gone to Richmond to picnic on the banks of the Thames. Adrian had wanted to drive Emma and Athene there in his curricle, but Mr Tenison had gently insisted that it would be better for them to accompany him and Mrs Tenison in their landau. Nick had also refused Adrian's offer of a seat and had chosen to ride instead, stabling his horse at a nearby inn before walking to the riverside, where he found the party already underway.

Servants were unpacking wicker baskets and laying out food and drink on lace-edged linen cloths. Adrian and Marcus were entertaining the women, Adrian having prevailed on Marcus to accept Nick's rejected seat. Adrian's driving had been so unsteady that Marcus had deeply regretted having accepted his invitation and had spent the journey trying to persuade Adrian not to set out yet on his proposed race to Brighton to break the record for the run.

Marcus was afraid that the only thing Adrian might break would be his neck and not the record! He was tactful enough not to say so, merely suggesting that Adrian needed a little more practice in driving a curricle and two.

Now he was listening to Emma saying in her low pretty voice, 'We thought that he had just come to question Papa about the murder, but he also wanted to interview Mama, Athene and me. Papa thought that it would be better to agree to him doing so rather than refuse him.'

Mr Tenison said quietly, 'I thought that to refuse might make it look as though we had something to hide.'

Nick, knowing that Jackson had recently been on an errand for him in the Steepwood district, but had not yet reported back, wondered what on earth the man was doing, and whether it had any connection with his own commission, and said, as calmly as he could, 'I can understand someone questioning you, sir, but why should he trouble the ladies? And who gave this man the authority to do so?'

'His name is Jackson,' said Mr Tenison. 'I understood from him that he wished to know whether anyone in my household had been friendly with the missing Marchioness and consequently might have some notion of where she could have gone—if she is still alive that is. The *on dit* is that her husband might have murdered her. As to the man's authority, he provided proof that he was working for the Home Office, and also for a very grand personage indeed. More I cannot say.'

Nick was fascinated by this answer. How many birds was the devious Jackson seeking to kill with one stone? And how soon would it be before he reported back to him anything which he might have discovered about Athene's origins?

'And could any of you help him?' he asked, directing his question to Emma and not to Athene, who was standing there quiet and demure.

'I couldn't,' she said, 'but Athene knew the Marchioness a little, I believe—but we understand that she couldn't help Mr Jackson.'

Athene had later learned that Jackson had told Mrs Tenison of her having been a friend of Louise's, and she had consequently been compelled to endure a stiff bout of questioning from her about the missing Marchioness.

Adrian snorted. 'If it isn't the outside of enough to have some great brute of a fellow questioning gentlewomen about their past friendships. I wonder you didn't have the vapours, Athene.'

He was so concerned and so vehement that Marcus Angmering gave him an odd look, thinking, so that's the way the wind blows, is it? It really is the incandescent companion he's after and not the demure young lady!

Athene thought to quieten matters down a little by saying, 'He wasn't a great brute, Adrian, and he was perfectly polite to me when questioning me. More polite, I might say, than some gentlemen I have known.'

If she gave a rapid glance in Nick's direction when she came out with this, Adrian failed to notice it, and exclaimed indignantly, 'If any gentleman is ever unkind to you in the future, Athene, you must inform me immediately and I shall soon mend his manners for him, you may be sure of that!'

'He was very polite to me, too,' said Emma. 'I was quite upset before I went in to see him, but he soon put me at ease, and Mama, too.'

'So you knew the Marchioness, Miss Filmer,' Marcus said. 'I have often wondered what the woman who chose to marry Sywell was like.'

There was no help for it, Athene thought ruefully. The last thing which she wished to do was discuss her friendship with Louise, but she could not refuse Marcus's unspoken question. It was quite natural that he should want to know something of the man—and his wife—whom it was suspected that his father might have killed. It would be unnatural for her not to say something.

'She was very young and very pretty,' she said slowly. 'We had been friends when I was a little girl, and then she was sent away—I never knew why, or to where. When the Marquis brought her to Steepwood I met her in the grounds one day and we renewed our friendship. She was lonely and seemed unhappy. She disappeared as suddenly as she had reappeared, and so I told Mr Jackson. I had no notion of where she went. That's all. I was sorry to lose a friend. We painted and sketched together, I'm afraid that I can't tell you any more.'

'Thank you, Miss Filmer. I trust that I have not distressed you. We none of us like to lose a friend.'

Athene nodded: Nick, like Jackson, cynically wondered whether she had told the whole story of her relationship with the Marchioness. He also wondered how long it would be before Jackson informed him of the results of his enquiry into Athene's origins. He would have dearly liked to have known what Jackson was really questioning Athene about.

'What is extraordinary,' he said slowly, 'is that so many of us, sitting here by the Thames and ready to enjoy the food and drink which the servants have set out for us, should have some involvement with Sywell and his missing wife.'

Adrian said, 'Well, I'm certainly glad that *I* never had anything to do with him. He sounds a most disagreeable person.'

'I think that we can all safely say Amen to that,' was Mr Tenison's final comment before he changed the subject and began talking about the other staple topic of conversation these days—the latest war news from Spain.

On the following afternoon Nick was reading in the drawing-room of his lodgings in Albany—which were not far from those which Lord Byron occupied—when his man ushered Jackson in.

The ex-Runner was looking uncommonly cheerful, which Nick hoped might be the consequence of an exceedingly fruitful foray into Northamptonshire. He thought to score a useful point or two before Jackson began his report by remarking dryly, 'I have been expecting you ever since I discovered that my little errand was not the only reason why you visited Steepwood recently.'

Oh, he was a fly boy, Mr Nick Cameron, was he not? Jackson rewarded him with a conspiratorial grin, and, 'So the Tenisons have been talking, have they?'

Nick nodded. 'And others, too. So, what did you unearth about Miss Filmer? Besides any possible clues to the fates of the murdered Marquis and the missing Marchioness, that is?'

'Something,' said Jackson, who thought that it usually paid to be honest. 'But not, perhaps, as much as you had hoped. There seems to be little doubt that she is illegitimate. She has a supposedly widowed mother who has behaved with impeccable virtue ever since she settled in Northamptonshire. The late Mr Filmer was unknown to the district, and none of his, or her, relatives have ever visited her during the twenty years since she settled there.

'I met a local gossip who implied with a nod and a wink that Miss F. is almost certainly illegitimate. After that I pursued other avenues, by which it came to my notice that her mother has been, and still is, in receipt of an annuity, paid quarterly, on a draft drawn on Coutts Bank—the name of the origin of the money being unknown. Regretfully, since with Coutts confidentiality for their customers is absolute, that is as far as I can take you. The annuity is not large, but has enabled the two women to live moderately well. As to who her father might be—that, I fear, is beyond discovery, since no one knows where Mrs Filmer lived before arriving in Steep Ride.

'Despite the rumours about Miss Filmer's birth, her mother is accepted by local society, teaches at the Sunday school and is known for being as charitable as her income will allow. There is one other thing of interest. Miss Filmer was a friend and confidante of the missing Marchioness of Sywell, and it is my belief that she is well aware of where that lady may be found—although she resolutely denies all knowledge of her whereabouts. Rumour has it that she is a clever young lady, and so I found her to be.'

So, Athene was illegitimate, some person of reasonable wealth's deserted bastard. Jackson's information explained much of her behaviour, and Nick suddenly felt a tremendous pity for her. What she was chasing was not only wealth, but respectability and acceptance. She must be aware of her mother's—and her own—precarious position in society. To marry Adrian would at once advance her to a position where she could out-stare the world.

'You are telling me, then,' said Nick carefully, 'that in some, perhaps distant way, Miss Filmer is involved in the Steepwood mystery.'

'Only to the extent that she may know where the Marchioness is. May I add that I believe that there is little more to be found about her, or her mother. The mother has been most remarkably discreet and I believe the young woman to be of a similar nature.'

He did not say that having met Athene he could not but admire her, but the suggestion was there.

'Do I understand that you regard your commission for me as at an end?'

'Indeed—unless you have any further information to offer me.'

Nick shook his head. 'None: so all that remains is for me to pay you, and thank you. I trust that your other investigations proved to be more successful than the one for me has been.'

It was Jackson's turn to shake his head.

'Alas, no. The business of the Marquis's murder is as mysterious as ever. Even if the Marchioness were to be found, it is doubtful whether she has any useful information.'

'You do not think that she *is* dead?'

'My instincts—which are seldom wrong—tell me

that she is not, particularly since I believe that Miss Filmer knows more than she is telling.'

'Miss Filmer always knows more than she is telling,' said Nick savagely, handing Jackson his guineas, and telling him to go to the kitchen where his man would give him a farewell tankard of porter.

He threw himself into his armchair—his book lay forgotten on the floor. One thing and one thing only was true—regardless of what Jackson had told him—whether Athene was legitimate or illegitimate, whether she was helping Louise Sywell or not, nothing had been solved for him.

He was like a man lost on the ocean in a row-boat without oars. Only one thing was certain, in honour he must not let Athene know that he had set Jackson to spy on her. Doubtless she thought the man had pursued her because of her relationship with Louise: that he had also pursued her on his behalf must remain, for the time being at least, his guilty secret.

'Will you accept Adrian if he offers for you?' Emma asked Athene one golden afternoon not long after Jackson had caused such a brouhaha in the Tenison household.

'What makes you think he will?' replied Athene. They were seated in the drawing-room, supposed to be engaged in canvas-work. Emma, however, had abandoned hers, and had been mooning over a novel before she had questioned Athene.

Now she said, 'It's the way he looks at you—full

of worship. I wondered, though, how you really felt about him. I don't think *you* worship *him*.'

This was perceptive for Emma, but then, she had grown very much more mature lately, and was no longer so ready to be stifled by her mother.

Athene thought for a moment before saying, 'Not exactly.'

'I thought not,' said Emma her voice wistful.

'But I like him,' said Athene hastily. After all, if she were to accept his offer, for despite what she had just said to Emma she thought that an offer was on the way, she must show some enthusiasm for marrying him.

The trouble was that lately, every time that she thought about what marriage really entailed, not just the going to bed bit, but also that one would have to spend one's days talking and engaging in the business of living with one's husband, the prospect of doing any of it with Adrian had become less and less attractive the more she knew him—and face it, Athene, the more she had come to know and appreciate Nick.

She could certainly spend her life talking to Nick— possibly disagreeing with him sometimes—sure that her days with him would always be lively. She preferred not to admit to herself that her nights might be livelier, too!

When once she had visualised marrying a man for his money and his title without thinking of everything else which that would entail, she was now thinking of the entail bit more and more and had begun to doubt whether she was cold-blooded enough to go through with it.

The worst of it was that she had, at first, done everything she could to attract Adrian to her, and now that she was no longer so welcoming Adrian had become so sure of her that he wasn't aware of how much her manner to him had cooled.

She wondered if Nick had noticed the change. Oh, bother everything—must she always be thinking of him? He had not been so unkind to her lately, but that was perhaps was because he was resigned to her marrying his cousin and did not wish to distress him.

Emma said suddenly. 'I wouldn't have thought Adrian to be best suited to you at all. I think he's dazzled by you rather than in love with you.'

Athene was surprised by her charge all over again. Emma's shrewd remark—which showed that she had inherited some of her father's sharp intelligence—added to the questions she was asking herself about her own behaviour towards Adrian.

Where once, if Adrian had asked her to marry him, she would have said yes to him on the instant, without further thought, she was now experiencing an increasing hesitancy. Which only went to show, she thought ruefully, how much practice differs from theory! Before she came to London she had felt no compunction at all about the prospect of marrying a man for his money and title, instead of for himself, but everything which had happened to her since she had set foot in the place had shown her what an innocent she must have been.

'He's a good man,' she said, as much to encourage herself as to explain her motives to Emma.

'And a good man deserves the best,' said Emma quietly, picking up her needlework again, before changing the subject by asking Athene to advise her on the best colour for the flower which she was working.

Athene looked across at her charge. Why all this worry from her about whether she and Adrian were suited to one another? Quick as a flash the obvious answer came. Emma was in love with him herself. He was exactly the sort of decent, slightly simple man with whom she would be happy, because she would ask little of him which he would be unable to give.

This insight had Athene feeling more disturbed than ever. She had not sufficiently prepared herself for the notion that her own activities, pursued to achieve her happiness, might cause unhappiness in others.

For the first time she began to understand why Nick Cameron was so critical of her, and to ask herself whether he might not have some right on his side.

The Duke of Inglesham was entertaining a visitor. Or, more correctly, he was receiving one whom he had summoned.

The ex-Bow Street Runner, Jackson, who had been recommended to him by no less a person than Lord

Liverpool, was standing deferentially before him, awaiting his instructions. In Jackson's experience such grand personages usually dealt with lesser lights like himself through their secretary or their flunkies. He wondered what it was that was so confidential that he was being received in person.

He was soon to find out, and what he was being asked came as some surprise to him—and brought a certain, hidden, amusement.

'I was told that you are discreet, and that I can rely upon you absolutely,' the Duke began, a trifle hesitantly. 'I would not care for my interest in this matter to be gossiped about. I would wish you to discover everything about the origins of a young lady and her mother who live in the Northamptonshire village of Steep Ride. When I say everything, I wish you to understand that, for me, the word means exactly what it says.'

Jackson nodded. 'Understood, Your Grace. Do not trouble yourself: the grave is no quieter than I am.'

Inwardly he was asking himself, what next? Did all roads lead to Steepwood these days, and was it, could it be, Miss Athene Filmer in whom the Duke was interested?

Indeed, it was. Out it all came, the Duke hemming and hawing as though the matter were some trifle— which Jackson was sure that it was not.

'I understand that Miss Filmer and her widowed mother have lived there since shortly after Miss Filmer was born. There are reasons, business reasons, which mean that I must have full knowledge of everything to do with them.'

Well, the ex-Runner was behaving like the Sphinx which Liverpool had said he was. He was listening, his head on one side, his craggy face gravely concentrating on every word that Inglesham was saying. The Duke was not to know that Jackson was debating with himself how truthful, how honest, he ought to be with his new master.

After all, he already knew everything that was to be known—other than the reason for the Duke's surprising interest—about the young lady and her mother. If he said nothing he could make another— cursory—visit to Steep Ride, and then return as though he had been urgently engaged on the Duke's business. Or he could inform the Duke of what he already knew, after telling him that his recent investigations about the Marquis of Sywell's murder, and his wife's disappearance, had led him indirectly to the Filmers. As a result he had seen fit to find out as much about them as he could. To do so, however, would probably mean that the Duke's fee would be less.

He said, slowly, after he had reluctantly decided on the latter, truthful, course, 'As it happens, Your Grace, quite by chance, I can inform you immediately of everything concerning the young lady and her mama.'

The Duke said sharply, 'How is that? They are not in trouble, I hope? Or under any suspicion?'

'Oh, no,' Jackson said, reassuringly, and went on

to explain to His Grace his commission from the Home Office and his discovery of the friendship of Miss Athene Filmer and the missing Marchioness. 'Just dotting all the i's and crossing all the t's as is my way—but to no purpose this time. The young lady denied all knowledge of the Marchioness's whereabouts.'

'Go on,' urged the Duke. So Jackson informed him of everything which he had told Nick Cameron, without mentioning Nick's name and his interest in Athene.

'Coutts,' said the Duke hollowly when the man had finished. 'The banker's draft came from Coutts.'

'Which, as you doubtless know, Your Grace, means that we have reached *point non plus.*'

'Yes,' said the Duke wearily. 'It would be as well if I knew further details of it, but what you have told me is sufficient to my purpose: I am sure I know who arranged it. You say the young lady is both beautiful and clever and that her mother has been chaste despite the rumours about her daughter's birth.'

'Indeed, Your Grace. I would be wasting your money if I returned there, since I believe that nothing further of use remains to be found in Northamptonshire.'

'Yes, and I see also that you are an honest man.'

The Duke went to a splendid ormolu desk, opened a drawer and took from it a full purse which he handed to Jackson. 'I am giving you what I intended to reward you with had it been necessary for you to visit Steepwood. Should I need to do so, I would not hesitate to employ you again.'

After Jackson had gone, the Duke, his face a picture of grief mixed with hope, walked over to the desk and fetched from a locked drawer a small miniature of a beautiful young woman dressed in the fashion of some twenty years before.

'I never thought to see you again,' he said, after kissing it, 'nor do I deserve to, but God may be kind and give me a second chance.'

Adrian had made up his mind. The Season was wearing on. He knew that Nick was dubious about the notion of his marrying Athene, and probably his mother might be, too. On the other hand she had never yet refused him anything, and when she saw how lovely and clever Athene was, she would be sure to approve of his choice.

The beauty of it was that by marrying her he could please himself and also give the Kinloch estates the heir which all his relatives were blithering about whenever they saw him.

Since she had no mother or father with her, he would do the proper thing and approach Mr Tenison first. He was never quite sure what the Tenisons thought of him. Mrs Tenison was always polite, but that might be because she wanted to catch him for Emma, who was a pretty little thing, but not Athene's equal.

Now had he not met Athene then Emma would

certainly have been his target. Partly because of that, he was not sure of Mr Tenison's approval of his choice of Athene. He was such a clever devil and had a way of looking at a fellow as though he were an insect on a pin. Well, it wasn't him he intended to marry, so what of that!

He came to these interesting conclusions on the night that they all visited Astley's. Marcus Angmering should have gone with them but he had cried off. 'I have to go into the country to see some relatives on my father's business,' he had said. 'A great bore, but there it is.'

Rumour said that Angmering also thought his father a great bore, but not so much of one that he suspected him of murder!

The following afternoon saw Adrian outside the Tenisons' home. He was dressed even more *à point* than usual, and his hair was a miracle of the hairdresser's art. It took him some minutes to summon up enough courage to order his driver to knock on the front door. He had not come in his curricle lest the journey spoil the perfection of his appearance.

Fortunately for Adrian's resolution Mr Tenison was neither out, nor engaged, and was prepared to see M'lord at once.

If Mr Tenison knew why Adrian, dressed to kill, wished to see him, he gave nothing away. He looked at the poor fellow in his usual searching manner, so that Adrian dismally concluded that whether or not he impressed Athene he had certainly not impressed her employer.

'I am at your service, m'lord,' was all Mr Tenison said.

'Yes, yes, indeed,' gabbled Adrian. 'I have approached you, sir, because Miss Filmer has no other relative or protector in London, and I felt that it would not be proper for me to propose marriage to her without asking the one person who might be thought to be her protector if I might approach her.'

'Very laudable of you,' said Mr Tenison dryly, somewhat astonished at the spectacle of Adrian coming out with a sentence which had so many words in it, and some of them long! Doubtless love was responsible for this achievement.

Adrian bowed, before saying eagerly, 'I may speak to her alone, then?'

'Only after I have informed her of the reason for your errand. I shall ask you to retire to the drawing-room, where I shall send her when I have told her why you are here.'

Everything was going swimmingly, Adrian thought, sitting in the pretty little room, waiting for his intended to arrive. He was sure that she *would* be his intended before he left the house. They had dealt so well together since they had first met that he could not believe that she would refuse him.

Upstairs Athene was listening to Mr Tenison informing her of Adrian's intention to propose to her. If ever she had thought that such a day might come, she had always imagined that she would immediately be over the moon with joy. Instead she did not know how she felt. Fright warred with delight. Now that the moment had come, could she really go through with it?

She tried to show as little emotion as possible while Mr Tenison was speaking, and he could not have guessed at the conflicting passions which consumed her.

Perhaps he did, though, a little, since before he dismissed her he said in his calm, kind way, 'You must have been aware, my dear, that His Lordship was about to propose, and I trust that you have given a great deal of thought to the answer you ought to give to him.'

Unaccountably Athene's eyes filled with tears. 'Oh, yes, I have,' she said simply. 'A great deal. Only...' and she fell silent until he prompted her by saying, 'Only, my dear...?'

'Only that when these things happen they often take on a very different complexion from when one merely thinks about them.'

He nodded his head. 'I know what you mean. I can only say to you, trust in your God and be true to yourself, Athene, and you cannot go wrong.'

She was holding these words in her mind when she faced a smiling Adrian downstairs. She knew at once that he was sure that she would accept him, and the panic which she felt at the idea of tying herself irrevocably to him surfaced again. More than that, she was frightened of hurting him, for had she not given him the impression that he meant more to her than he actually did, so that he was taking her acceptance for granted?

His first words told her that she was right on that count.

'Oh, Athene, you must know why I have come—even if old Tenison hadn't told you why I am here, you surely would have known. I cannot live without you, and my dearest wish is that you should become my wife as soon as we can arrange the marriage.'

He was so full of innocent delight that he fell on one knee before her and took her cold hands in his to kiss them.

Be true to yourself, Mr Tenison had said, and in order to do that she must not let Adrian go any further until she had told him the whole truth *about* herself.

His smile slowly disappeared when she did not immediately answer him, but loosed her hands gently from his and said, 'Oh, Adrian, before you say anything more there is something which I have to tell you.'

'No need for that,' he said, smiling again. 'All that you need to say is yes.'

Athene shook her head and said, stiff-lipped, 'I must tell you, Adrian, that I am not legitimate. Worse than that, I have no notion of who my father might be. Can it be possible that your family would agree to your marrying someone who has no right to the name which she bears? Someone who has no fortune and no known relatives?'

To do him justice, he showed no signs that he was shocked. He simply said, 'My darling Athene, it is you whom I wish to marry, not your father, nor your mother. What you have just told me makes no difference to my feelings for you. I repeat again, will you marry me?'

If she accepted him now it would be for two reasons, neither of them satisfactory. The first reason would be because of his unthinking generosity in not allowing her dubious social position to weigh with him, the second would be that she would say yes out of pity, not wishing to hurt him when he had been so good and kind.

Reason told her, yes, he can say he would marry you, despite all, now, at this minute, but later—how will he feel later when the vile gossip begins, as it surely will. I can only accept him if I truly love him, but if I am honest I cannot say that. I like him, yes, but, given everything, liking is not enough.

The longer she hesitated the more his honest face began to cloud over. 'I had not thought that you would refuse me,' he muttered sadly. 'I thought that you felt for me what I feel for you.'

She would try to let him down lightly, find some form of words which might delay things, give him time to think over the enormity of what she had told him. To have told him the truth might cost her everything, but at least it was one less lie on her conscience.

'Adrian,' she said simply, 'I am not sure exactly what my feelings for you are, and I'm also not certain what yours are for me. If I suggested to you that you give us both a little time before you require an answer from me, then we can consider most carefully whether we really wish to marry one another.'

He shook his head. 'I already know that I wish to marry you.'

'Ah, but does not my hesitation tell you that we might be reading one another wrongly?'

By his puzzled face it was clear that this was beyond him. Athene thought ruefully that Nick would have known immediately what she had meant, and that pinpointed the difference between the two men, and the reason why she was now hesitating about accepting Adrian's offer.

'Think,' she told him gently. 'We lose nothing by waiting a little, say a week. It will give us an opportunity to get to know one another even more than we do.'

'I know you well enough already,' he said stubbornly, 'to know that I want you for my wife.'

'I haven't refused you,' Athene said, now a little desperate. 'Only asked you to wait a little for an answer.'

'You promise to give me one soon? I do not need a week, but I will accept that.'

'Indeed, I would not keep you forever on the end of a piece of string.'

This provoked the ghost of a chuckle from him. 'No, indeed. I cannot think that in the end you will refuse me.'

'And we shall not speak of this to anyone?'

'If that is what you wish.'

'I do wish it. For the moment it must remain our secret.'

It was over. He kissed her hand and bowed to her, his face melancholy, leaving Athene standing there, alone, among the ruins of all that she had schemed for, ever since she had first known she was going to London with the Tenisons.

Mr Tenison had told her to be true to herself, and so she had: but what might it cost her?

CHAPTER SEVEN

'I've done it, Nick. Popped the question—it was easier than I thought. She wants a week to think my proposal over, and she did ask me to keep it a secret, but I can't think that it would trouble her if I told you—and no one else of course.'

'Of course,' echoed Nick mechanically. 'I take it that you are speaking of Athene Filmer.'

'Who else? Mind you, I was in the boughs until she asked for a week to consider it, but I can't believe that she will refuse me. Women like to keep you on a string, you know.'

'So they do,' said Nick, his mind reeling from the knowledge that Athene, after what he considered her careful campaign, had not immediately accepted Adrian. She must have some ulterior motive for refusing to accept him at once—but whatever could it be? To keep him dangling would reinforce her power over him, but she was risking a possible change of mind from his cousin. He could scarcely believe that she would do other than accept him joyfully at the end of the week.

'You are sure that you are prepared for your mama's shock that you have not proposed to one of the golden dollies who are on offer this Season?'

He did not tell Adrian of his discovery of Athene's low birth, because to do so would have betrayed the fact that he had set spies on the trail of the woman his cousin loved. And what would that do to their long-standing friendship?

'No, thank you, I wouldn't have a golden dolly as a gift. They are so taken up with all their riches that they think that they are doing you a favour by marrying you.'

'There is that,' agreed Nick.

He could not explain why he felt so numb at the prospect of Pallas Athene's marriage to Adrian. He had a sudden burning wish to confront her with his knowledge of her origins and of how she was tricking Adrian, and at the same time, yet another contrary wish—never to see her again: it would be too painful.

'You seem a little glum, old fellow. I thought that you'd be happy for me. Congratulations are in order, you know.'

'Not until she has actually said yes,' returned Nick, who had just made a sudden decision to leave London and visit his sister in Hampshire who was constantly complaining that she saw him so seldom.

But not before he had had a last interview with Athene.

* * *

'Oh, Louise, I have so much to tell you. My life has become so complicated that I often think sadly back to the peace of Steep Ride: a peace which I wished to escape, but now that I have, oh dear...' and Athene did something her friend had never seen before.

She burst into tears.

'Come, come. This is not like you, my dear,' said Louise tenderly, putting an arm about her weeping friend.

'I know. I'm usually brave. I can never remember crying before, but whatever choice I make, and I need to make one, seems to me to be a wrong one.'

She had found time somehow to visit Louise in order to warn her of Jackson's busy-bodying around Steepwood, which could constitute a threat to her anonymity if he discovered where she was, and also to ask for her advice over Adrian's proposal.

Where to start? In fairness to Louise she ought to begin by telling her of Jackson, so, sniffling occasionally, she did.

'I hope that I gave nothing away, but I could tell that he did not believe me.'

'If you denied everything then all he has is guesswork.'

'True,' Athene said, 'but I nearly didn't visit you, because I am terrified that I might be followed. I brought a big bag with me—as you see—with another shawl and bonnet in it, and when I was well away from Chelsea I changed into them, stuffing what I had been wearing into the bag so that I should be difficult to identify from a distance.'

Louise said admiringly, 'You would make a good conspirator, Athene.'

Athene sniffled again. 'Nick Camcron would say that I am well named. The goddess was cunning, too.'

Nick's was a new name for Louise to remember. She had heard of Adrian Kinloch before, but little of anyone else.

She said, 'If you are telling me the truth, and I know you are, he cannot trace me through you. I shouldn't worry about Jackson unduly. Is that all which is troubling you? It scarcely seems worth so many tears!'

This small sally set Athene smiling tremulously.

'No, it's not that. It's just...just...that Lord Kinloch has proposed to me and I don't know what answer to give him. I told him yesterday that I'd give him one in a week, and I haven't the faintest notion what my answer will be.'

'Is that the Kinloch who owns a third of Scotland?' Louise asked.

'Yes. He's exactly the sort of person who, before I came to London, I hoped might offer for me: he's handsome, immensely rich and has a title—what more could a poor girl wish for? I have to confess that I encouraged him from the moment we met—he seemed interested in me straight away.'

'I don't understand why you can't make up your

mind to accept him. He certainly sounds like someone any girl would want, let alone a poor one.'

'Oh, Louise, it's not as simple as that—it's just that he's such a simple creature. He's like a friendly puppy, I like him very much as a sort of kind friend, but the idea of marrying him frightens me because, if I am honest, we have nothing in common. I'm not even sure that he really loves me. My charge, Emma Tenison, has suggested that I dazzle him. What happens when that wears off? When he discovers that we have nothing in common? That everything which interests me, bores him? If I marry him it will be because he's rich Lord Kinloch—and anything more mercenary than that, I cannot imagine. How can I be true to myself *and* marry him?'

Louise said slowly, 'You don't love him at all? Not at all? It would then be a kind of arranged marriage— an odd one, which you have arranged for yourself?'

'Yes. I mean, no, no, I don't love him. You have put it perfectly.'

Louise leaned forward, grasped Athene's hand and looked her in the eye. 'My dear, all that I can say to you is this. It is not for me to decide for you, but I made the mistake of marrying Sywell mostly because I needed to feel safe, to gain a place in the world. Oh, he showed me his best side—which he discarded once we were married—but I must face the fact that to some extent we deceived one another. You understand me. Lord Kinloch doesn't sound like Sywell, but there are many ways of being unhappy.'

Athene kissed Louise on the cheek. 'You are a good creature and I will bear what you have said in mind.'

'Excellent, and now, because you have been honest with me, I will be honest with you. I, too, might be illegitimate, as you have told me that you are, but I cannot prove whether I am or not. More than that, if I am legitimate, then I have a claim to be considered a member of one of the great families of England: a member who has been cheated of all her rights of birth.'

She paused, and Athene said, her brave spirits rapidly returning, 'Oh, we are a sorry pair, are we not? I am almost beginning to believe that all of us who live in and around Steepwood Abbey are indeed cursed.'

'Indeed we are, and like you, I am beginning to believe in the curse—however much I wish not to,' said Louise. 'My story is very similar to yours, except that there is this strong possibility that my father did marry my mother. He was the Yardley family's black sheep, Rupert Cleeve, Viscount Angmering, the seventh Earl's heir. He went to France in the middle of their Revolution, convinced that the reformers there were about to transform the world. When it began to turn violent, he and the young Frenchwoman with whom he had fallen in love travelled back to England. Either before they left, or afterwards, he married her.

'What my father had not reckoned with was my grandfather's behaviour when he learned that my mother, Marie de Ferrers, was a Catholic. For some reason my grandfather detested them, why, my father never knew. The Earl's first action on learning of my mother's religion was to disinherit his son, which he could do because the estate was not entailed, and banish him from the family home.

'I was told that my father left England for France vowing never to return until his wife was accepted. As it happened neither of them had long to live: my mother died of a wasting disease and my father was killed in one of the Parisian bread riots in 1793. After their deaths all their letters and papers disappeared. My guardian, John Hanslope, who was the Yardleys' bailiff, believed that my grandfather destroyed them so that his son's daughter—myself—would have no claim to be recognised as a legitimate member of the family, preferring everything go to a distant cousin, leaving me without so much as a halfpenny for my dowry.

'My guardian was convinced that my parents were married, but could find no proof that such a ceremony had ever taken place. So, there you have it. Not only was I Sywell's unconsidered wife, but I am also the Yardleys' abandoned Lady Louise, reduced to earning a living as a country seamstress and then as a London *modiste*.'

The two young women stared at one another, and then, improbably, they began to laugh.

'If I read such a farrago as I have just told you in a Minerva Press novel,' said Louise at last, after wiping her eyes, 'I would say that it was the most immense nonsense, but my guardian, a most down-to-earth man, swears that it is all true.'

'My employer, Mr Tenison, once told me that real life is much more improbable than anything which one might find in a romantic story, so I have no difficulty in believing every word you say.'

'As I believe in yours.'

'I,' said Athene, 'have no claim to legitimacy, but if your parents did marry some evidence must exist somewhere. A proper search ought to be made. A man like Jackson would surely be able to track it down.'

'I can't afford him yet,' Louise told her. 'Everything I earn at present goes into my living expenses and into the business; little is left over. One day soon things will improve, but until then…' and she gave an elegant shrug of the shoulders which did much to convince Athene of her French origin.

Athene was still thinking things over when she reached Chelsea. It was her day off, and Mrs Tenison and Emma were out with Lady Dunlop paying duty calls, so she repaired to the library and amused herself by pulling down one of Mr Tenison's legal folios and looking through it for anything which might help Louise.

She was deep in a learned discussion relating to the laws of entail when the butler came in, looking somewhat disapproving.

'Mr Nicholas Cameron has just arrived, Miss Filmer, and is asking to speak to you. I told him that you were alone this afternoon, but he insisted that I should ask you if you will receive him for a few moments.'

Athene hesitated. She was well aware that it was quite against the rules for a single young woman to entertain a man alone, and she could not help wondering why Nick wished to see her. Could Adrian have informed him of his proposal? Yes, that seemed the most likely explanation. He had probably come to bully her again, to insist that she should not accept him.

Even so she suddenly made her mind up.

'You may tell Mr Cameron that I will receive him here, in the library, but for a few moments only.' The butler's face grew even more disapproving on receiving this order, but he left to do as he was bid.

His expression, however, was less forbidding than the one Nick was wearing when he entered.

Goodness! She was right. He *had* come to hector her. Athene put her hands behind her back, stood straight and tall before the map of the world which covered part of one wall, and stared bravely back at him. She did not offer him a seat.

'Yes, Mr Cameron, what is it you want?'

He was as stiff as she was and bowed to her as though she were a stranger.

'It is perhaps no business of mine but I understand that my cousin has proposed to you...'

Athene could not prevent herself: she interrupted him, her voice icy. 'You are right, it is no concern of yours. But, pray continue, I am all agog to hear what you have to say on the matter.'

'This: I understand that you are keeping him dangling, whether for a genuine reason or to demonstrate your power over him, or perhaps because you prefer to wait for a better offer of some sort from Inglesham.' He paused.

She had no notion of how the mere sight of her, standing there beautiful, proud and tall, affected him. Frustration drove him on. 'What I do know is that you have, so far, successfully deceived the world as to your origins. What would he have to say to you if he knew that you are…'

Nick stopped. He could not say it, could not imagine how he could have the sheer folly, nay, the cursed brutality, to come here to twit her with her ignoble birth—of which he must have learned by ignoble means. Every vestige of colour had fled from her face, but she was as calm and still in her beauty as the goddess who presided over the Old Bailey, as calm and still as Pallas Athene herself. Despite all, he could not but admire her.

'Yes,' she said, 'pray continue—I am sure that there is more to come. It would be a pity to waste your journey here, would it not?'

Calm she might appear to be, but her heart was bleeding. Oh, she might deserve reproach for her campaign to catch Adrian, but not from him, never from him—that she could not bear. She could outface the whole world, but not him.

And he must never know that.

'Very well,' he said, for having begun he must go on to the end, however bitter it might be. 'That you are, to put it kindly, nameless.'

He stopped again.

'Say it,' she said. 'That I am illegitimate. Does the word frighten you? It no longer frightens me. Nor did it frighten Adrian when I told him. If I accept him he will take me as I am, illegitimate and fatherless. So, Mr Nicholas Cameron, your errand is a waste of time. Whether I marry Lord Kinloch—or not—the decision is mine to make, not yours, never yours. I will not ask you how you came by this knowledge—but I can guess.'

What to say? That she was honest—more honest than he had dared to hope—and had risked all by confessing all. That Adrian was nobler, or more foolish than he was. That he was a cur beyond belief to arrive in the home where she might consider herself safe and try to blackmail her? Yes. However he might dress up what he had tried to do, blackmail it was.

'I am sorry,' he said. 'I might have known...'

Athene wanted to weep and scream. So he had always thought her a selfish, scheming harpy, and gone was any hope that she had ever nursed that he might see her as she was: young, helpless, alone in a world where her kind had no hope of betterment save through the man that they might marry—as she might marry Adrian.

All he had succeeded in doing was the opposite of what he had intended. She had been ready to refuse Adrian, to assert her better self, but since Nicholas Cameron and the world believed that she had no better self, she would accept Adrian.

'Known what? That I was not the scheming adventuress you thought me? Know this, Mr Nicholas Cameron. Before you came to see me I had made up my mind not to marry your cousin, but you have changed that mind. If I have, with you, the reputation of being little better than the poor women who walk the streets and who sell themselves for gain, then I might as well live up to it. I have nothing more to say to you. You may leave, or not, as you please, but I shall not remain in the room with you any longer. I have my reputation as a future countess to consider.'

By God, she was a prize worth winning, and he, what had he done? In his blind folly he had thrown her away—nay, thrown her into his cousin's arms, for he was sure that she was telling the truth. She was as unlike Flora Laxford as a woman could be.

He made to move towards her, but she shrank away from him, whispering, 'Go, please go. We have nothing more to say to one another.'

Nick hesitated for a moment.

And then left, his world about his ears.

No one could have guessed, from the face Athene presented to society, the misery which consumed her.

What hurt her the most was that not only did Nick think so little of her that he could believe she would deceive Adrian about the circumstances of her birth, but that he must also have set the Runner, Jackson, on her trail. Was that why Jackson had been so urgent in his questioning of her? Did Nick believe that because her birth was dubious then all her actions would be tainted, that he could think she might know more of the Marquis of Sywell's dreadful end than she was telling him?

At least Nick had not taunted her with that, but what he had implied was bad enough.

He had twitted her with Inglesham, though, and perhaps, given the Duke's interest in her, that was not surprising. It was ironic that later in the day she and the Tenisons were due to attend the grand reception which the Duke was giving in his London palace off the Strand—one of the few remaining there.

All the ton were invited, and since this was his first entertainment for nearly fifteen years all the ton had accepted. Adrian was there, and danced attendance on her, his eyes following her everywhere so that he was chaffed by all the young men of his set. Only Nick was absent.

'And why the devil has he cried off?' Adrian complained to a friend. 'Only the devil knows. He was talking about coming only yesterday. He thought he might be given a chance to inspect the Duke's library, Lord knows why he should want to.'

'Supposed to be a grand one,' laughed Freddie Marchmont. 'Odd fellow, Nick, sometimes.'

'Deuced odd all the time lately,' grumbled Adrian, who had not forgiven Nick's lukewarm reception of his proposal to Athene. He thought that she was looking a bit peaky tonight: another problem for him. One might have believed that a girl proposed to by an Earl would look happier and not keep him waiting. For the first time in his pursuit of her Adrian was beginning to have second thoughts.

So, he had not the courage to face me here tonight, was Athene's explanation of Nick's absence, and she was not far wrong. Not only was he ashamed of his recent attempted interference in her affairs, but he was also beginning to tire of his idle life in the capital.

His father had wished him to take part in the Season as a social preparation for a future political life. The Cameron family had the power to send an MP to Parliament, and as the present incumbent was growing old, Mr Anthony Cameron thought that his clever son would make a useful successor. His reason for wanting Nick at Westminster would be so that he could put forward moderate proposals for land reform which would make it unnecessary for the Camerons to follow the Duke of Sutherland's policies in carrying out the Highland Clearances.

Not only did Nick's father wish to avoid the obloquy and hate which would follow such harsh measures, but he felt that he had a duty towards his tenants to try to avoid such a drastic action except as a last desperate resort to save his estates. Nick, having seen the narrow existence of his father's tenants, often felt ashamed of his own luxurious life in society.

When this was added to his unhappiness over Athene it became almost intolerable. He decided to visit his twin sister, who had married a Hampshire squire and was always complaining that she seldom saw him, and then return to London for a short time before going back to Scotland.

Consequently, on arrival at Albany after his disastrous interview with Athene he immediately arranged matters so that he could travel to Hampshire on the morrow, in the hope that a visit there might lighten the burden of misery under which he now laboured.

Whoever would have thought that a woman could affect him so!

Athene was affected too. The Season, which she had begun with such high hopes, had lost all its savour. Whenever she met Adrian he offered her a wounded face. His pride had been damaged by her refusal to accept him immediately. To try to salve his misery, he began to avoid her and to talk to Emma instead—much to Mrs Tenison's delight.

Nick's disappearance also distressed her more than she could have anticipated. Her days became wearisome and her evenings the more so. The only thing which lightened them were the letters from her mother detailing all the serio-comic happenings of the

Steepwood district, including a description of Jackson's visit.

'Apparently,' she wrote, 'I was the only person whom he didn't interview, which makes me either distinguished, or undistinguished, I'm not sure which.'

Athene had a sad chuckle over that, remembering Jackson's quizzing of her. One morning, just before the week she had promised Adrian was over, she received a thicker budget of letters than usual.

'Goodness,' exclaimed Emma, whose own budget that morning was light, 'you are lucky. I don't receive many letters and I do so adore reading them.'

'These are only from mother, and two old friends, one of whom is getting married. I think. Oh, and another, official-looking one. Goodness knows who that is from.' She essayed a mild joke. 'My banker, perhaps.'

Athene didn't open her letters immediately but took them to her room. One of the friends who had written to her was Louise, but, naturally, she hadn't seen fit to tell Emma of that. The official-looking letter she left to the last, even though it had aroused her curiosity.

She opened it carefully, to discover that it was from a firm of solicitors: Hallowes, Bunthorne and Thring. It was short and to the point and left her bewildered.

'Dear Madam,' it said. 'Pursuant to a matter of some urgency which has recently arisen we must ask you, of your goodness, to visit our office tomorrow at two o'clock of the afternoon, so that this matter may be resolved immediately.

'We must also urge you to keep this letter, and the visit, confidential. We assure you that nothing in the case concerned is to your detriment, and our reputation is such that I am sure that you are aware that you need have no fear that yours would suffer if you were to accede to our request...'

What in the world was all that about! If the matter concerning her was so serious—and so urgent—why had they not written to her mother? Her mother had said nothing in this morning's letter which could bear on this. Should she ignore them and seek Mr Tenison's advice as to whether she ought to visit 'our office' when the reason for the visit was cloaked in mystery?

Why should she ask Mr Tenison? Was not she, Athene Filmer, well able to determine her own fate? Had she not, this very week, in some sense or other seen off both Adrian and his cousin Nick? If she had been mistaken in her dealings with them, then the mistake was at least hers and no one else's.

She would go to the lawyers, Hallowes, Bunthorne and Thring—and of course she had heard of them, as who in the ton had not? She gave a nervous little laugh after thinking what pompous names they were.

She wondered what the owners of them were like, and what they had to do with her. Well, she would soon find out.

* * *

'I received this letter yesterday,' Athene said, showing it to the porter who sat in a little sentry box in the porch of the lawyers' offices, 'and I am here as requested.'

The porter fetched out a battered notebook and consulted it. 'You are Miss Athene Filmer?'

'Indeed, this letter is proof.'

'Follow me, madam, you are expected.'

The room she was shown into was so grand that Athene stared about her in amazement. The porter motioned her to a chair before disappearing through a pair of double doors, to emerge a few minutes later to usher her into what was obviously the firm's main office.

Inside, a little sharp-faced man who had been sitting at a desk as large as a billiard table rose to greet her with a low bow when the porter announced, 'Miss Filmer to see you, Mr Hallowes.'

'Miss Filmer, I see that you are prompt as to time,' he said, 'and your presence here is indeed a pleasure.'

Athene bowed back. 'I must say, sir, that for me this is rather more a surprise than a pleasure.'

He gave a short laugh at that. 'I was informed that you were a clever young woman. My information was obviously correct. You have kept this meeting confidential, I trust.'

'With a little difficulty, sir. My invention was taxed somewhat by having to find a convincing excuse to leave my employer's home this afternoon, but not so completely that I was unable to do so. I would be pleased to learn from you what this urgent business is which brings me here.'

He laughed a little at that, before saying, 'My dear Miss Filmer, it is not I who have business with you. I am merely an intermediary. I must ask you to accompany me to our private suite where, I assure you, everything will be explained.'

'It seems, sir, that I have no alternative but to obey you, since my curiosity is stronger than my commonsense.'

This elicited another chuckle from him.

'Very good, Miss Filmer, very good, indeed, but have no fear of what you may discover.'

He rose, saying, 'Pray take my arm, Miss Filmer. All will shortly be explained.'

He led her to another pair of double doors, along a short corridor lined with caricatures of legal figures and into a room which was so superbly furnished that it might have been found in the home of a Duke. So it was perhaps not surprising that a Duke should be present in it.

It was the Duke of Inglesham who rose to his feet to bow to them. Mr Hallowes relinquished Athene's arm and said, also bowing low, 'Your Grace, as you requested, Miss Filmer is here to see you. I will leave her with you, since that is your pleasure and your command.'

'Only if Miss Filmer agrees. You may rest assured,' the Duke said to her, bowing again, 'that your presence here is known to no one outside these prem-

ises. Mr Hallowes is aware of the reason why I have
sent for you, and should you, at any time, wish to
terminate our conference you are free to leave this
room—and the premises—immediately. I should
wish, however, that you would do me the honour of
hearing me out.'

Goodness, what in the world could all this be
about? thought the dazed Athene as Mr Hallowes
bowed himself from the room as though he were leaving royalty. When the door had shut behind him the
Duke waved a hand at an armchair. 'Pray be seated,
Miss Filmer. I shall stand, for what I have to say to
you must be said with all due consequence, not from
a man lounging in a chair.'

Since there was nothing else for it, Athene sat
down, but not before saying, 'I cannot help, Your
Grace, but wonder what you have to tell me, rather
than my mother. I am, after all, a single young woman
of little consequence, and it would be more natural
for you to approach me through her.'

'True. Very true. You are, however, a young
woman of great common-sense and presence of mind,
and what you have to say to me when I have finished
speaking will determine whether or not I approach
your mother.'

If, as I am beginning to suspect, thought Athene,
still bewildered, he is about to propose to me, as Nick
Cameron suggested the other day, then it would
surely be expected that he would apply to my mother
first, not last. On the other hand he is a noted eccen-

tric, and this might be just one more demonstration of his oddity.

'If that is so, Your Grace, then I will listen carefully to what you have to say.'

'Excellent,' he murmured, and although what she had just said seemed to have pleased him, he suddenly seemed oddly ill at ease before he began to speak.

'The events of which I am about to tell you occurred before you were born. I was then the heir to a Dukedom and an estate impoverished by my grandfather, who had squandered his enormous fortune on building a great house, and on gambling, drink and women. My father succeeded to a much reduced inheritance. Naturally, as a very young man, this meant little to me. My father was extremely friendly with the Rector of the parish church at Inglesham, and in the year before I went to Oxford I was sent to him to improve my scanty knowledge of Latin and Greek. My tutor had been remiss in educating me in the classics, preferring field sports to indoor bookishness— his phrase.

'The Rector had a pretty daughter of my own age— I was then seventeen, and we became great friends. She joined me in my studies and being with her made them easier for me—I was not about to let a young girl best me, you understand.

'She bested me in another way, for when I first came down from Oxford in the summer vacation I found that she had turned into a rare beauty, such a rare beauty that I immediately lost my heart to her.

I behaved myself, though, while I was at Oxford, telling myself that when my scholastic education there was over I should be able to ask her to be my wife.

'I was such a simpleton that it never occurred to me that there could be any objection to my marrying her. After all, her father was my father's best friend, he came from an old gentry family, impoverished it was true, but the name was one famous in the history of our country and has become more famous since. It was Nelson.

'I shall never forget that last summer when I came down from Oxford for the last time. We roved the woods around Inglesham together, secure in our happiness. Charlotte did once suggest that my father might not completely approve of our marrying, but I could not believe that he would refuse me. One day, when we were alone together—and it was, God forgive me, the only time that it happened—our gentle love-making turned into real passion and we forgot ourselves in fulfilling it.

'Now I knew that, in honour, I must seek my blessing from my father so that we might be married as soon as possible. Imagine my distress and horror when after I had told him of my love he informed me that there could be no question of my marrying a relatively poor young woman, however good her birth. The only thing which could save Inglesham from being lost to the family which had owned it since the Conquest was for me to make a rich marriage—which he was in the process of arranging with the daughter of a London merchant grown rich through the India trade.

'I argued and swore at him. I had been a good son who had always obeyed him without question and yet the first time I had ever asked anything from him he had refused me. Alas, he was adamant. If I did not agree to marry the woman he had chosen for me he would cast me off without a penny. Since the estate was not entailed it would go to a distant cousin and I would be left with only a worthless title when he died.

'In the middle of this my darling's father came to Inglesham Court to tell my father that his daughter was expecting my child. If I had thought that this would weaken my father's resolve, I was mistaken. He was more than ever determined that I should not marry a girl who had allowed me such freedom before marriage. Worse than that, my Charlotte's father agreed with him. We were both to be cast out into the world penniless if we did not give one another up.

'Were we to part, he and my father would fund a small annuity for my Charlotte, and see her settled in another part of the country as the unfortunate widow of the war then beginning, so that she might live a decent and respectable life. I, of course, was to marry the rich citizen's daughter my father had chosen for me. We were not to be allowed to meet again—unless we were so foolish as to try to elope together. Had we met, things might have been different...

'God forgive me, the two men wore me down. I gave up my dearest love without so much as a word of farewell. I had no notion of where she had gone, and I was made to promise that I would not try to find her or the child: I never knew whether it was a boy or a girl. I was well served for my cowardice. My wife was a shrew and we never had a child of our own. I had gained the whole world—for her money restored Inglesham and its estates to their former glory—but I had lost my soul. Had I my time again I would not have done what I did.

'I never knew another happy moment. What my life would have been if I had married Charlotte and abandoned everything I shall never know. What I do know is that to marry for money when one might marry for love is the worst thing anyone can do. The Bible said it once and for all: "Better is a dinner of herbs where love is, than a stalled ox and hatred therewith." I do not blame my wife for our unhappy marriage: I blame myself for agreeing to it.

'When she died I thought to look for your mother, but the trail was cold. Coutts would not give me details of the trust set up for her, if there were one. The Rector and his wife left the parish shortly after Charlotte was sent away, and I had no notion where they went. I had given up hope of ever finding her again until the night I saw you in the ballroom. I could not believe that two women could be so alike and not be related. I made it my business to find out all I could about you, and thanks to mere chance, the chance which rules all our lives, I discovered where your mother lives and that you are indeed my daughter.

'All that remains is to ask your forgiveness.'

Athene, who had been twisting her hands together in anguish as her father's sad tale unrolled, particularly when he had spoken of the folly of marrying for money, and not for love, said, 'From what you have told me you have suffered greatly—which must be punishment enough. My mother suffered, too, and still does. But why have you not told *her* this? Why me?'

'Because I am still a coward. I was, I am, fearful that she might hate me for my desertion of her—for that is what it must have seemed. I was fearful of what she might have told you. To tell you myself seemed to be the best way back for me. You are a clever young woman, compassionate, too. I have seen that pretty child of the Tenisons blossom under your care.'

'A way back,' murmured Athene. 'My mother never uttered a word of reproach about your desertion of her, leaving her to have a love child, and to be the object of malicious rumour. She never told me the name of her lover, and she said that she understood what pressures had been brought to bear on you to desert her. One day, before she was sent away from her home, and all she knew, from the home where she had been kept a prisoner, she packed a bag and tried to go to the byway where she knew that you rode daily in order to speak to you, to ask you to defy the world with her, but my grandfather caught her and stopped her, so she never tried again. He deserves forgiveness—if he still lives, that is. She never told me your name, or her own true one, and I have never met any of her family—which is mine also.'

'We are all sinful and all deserve forgiveness,' said the Duke tiredly. 'But if I were to meet your mother again, do you believe that she would not turn me away?'

'I think not—but would it not be fitting that you risked her doing so?'

'I think that you have your mother's courage and something of the shrewdness which all the Ingleshams are supposed to possess—except for my grandfather, of course. I now know where she lives and in due course I will visit her. The rest lies with God.'

Athene nodded. What her father had confessed to her had struck home. If she were now to marry Adrian was she not about to repeat what he had done and condemn herself to a barren, unhappy life when Adrian was no longer dazzled by her, and his shallowness bored her? The Duke had simply told her in different words what Mr Tenison had said to her on the day when Adrian had come to propose.

Whatever her brave and defiant words to Nick, she

would now refuse Adrian, and tell her father to try his fortune with her mother.

More she could not say or do.

CHAPTER EIGHT

'What in the world is wrong with you, Nick? You are like a bear with a sore head. Even Chudleigh has noticed that you are not your usual cheerful and cynical self, and you know how unobservant he usually is about everything other than the management of the estate and his family.'

Nick frowned. He had been trying not to read the *Morning Post* in case it contained an announcement of Athene and Adrian's coming marriage, when his sister had arrived to disturb his peace.

'Nothing, Lucy, nothing at all.'

His sister sat down opposite to him at the breakfast table, where he sat among the ruins of an insubstantial breakfast. This was simply another sign that something was amiss, since his love of food while remaining thin was a Cameron family joke.

'Don't try to bam me, Nick. It's your sister speaking and I always know when you are not telling the truth. What is it: is a woman troubling you?'

This was another family joke. There had always been a psychic bond between the pair of them. When one was struck, or hurt themselves when either together or apart, the other always cried as well.

Nick shrugged before giving a despairing laugh. 'What a witch you are, Lucy. I might have known that even after a long absence you still have the ability to read my mind. Yes, you're right, it *is* a woman.'

'And is she right for you, Nick? Is that why you are troubled—that she might not be?'

He groaned. 'Yes…no…I don't know. In any case she's going to marry Adrian. He's already proposed to her and he's only waiting for her to say yes.'

Lucy stared at him. 'You mean that he's met someone who didn't immediately fall into his arms? Goodness me, is she very rich, then, that she can afford to turn him down? All that lovely money and a title, too, must surely make up for his lack of brains.'

'That, my love, is the trouble. She's as beautiful as sin, as clever as the devil, as poor as a church mouse, and came to town to snare a rich husband, preferably one with a title. She's made him wait for an answer, one can't imagine why.'

'What I don't understand, Nick, is given all that, why she didn't immediately fall into his arms.' Lucy paused and added somewhat slyly, 'I suppose the cleverness, added to the beauty, is why you are taken with her. Does that have something to do with her making Adrian wait?'

'Yes, and the devil of it is, that on top of that, rich

though Adrian is, he's not as rich as Inglesham, and the *on dit* is that either she's after him, or he's after her. One can only suppose that she's holding Adrian off in order to see whether Inglesham proposes. After all a real live Duke, even if middle-aged, must be the catch of any Season.'

'I see. What I also see is that she must be something remarkable to have you all in such a pother over her.'

'Oh, yes,' said Nick bitterly. 'It's not often that one meets a man's brain in a beautiful woman's body. Everything she says and does is to perfection.'

He nearly added, 'Damn her,' but thought, better not.

'Oh, dear, Nick, you have got it badly, haven't you? What I don't understand is why you didn't propose to her yourself if she's such a nonpareil—if a female can be a nonpareil, that is.'

'I believe they can. But I have antagonised her too much for any proposal from me to succeed, and in the doing I have fallen even more utterly under her spell. We parted at odds and to be truthful we have never been at evens. I know what I feel for her: what I don't know is what she feels for me. I always laughed at fellows who mooned after a particular woman, but I assure you that I am not laughing now.'

'So I see. You suppose her to be mercenary, and after Flora Campbell's betrayal, that irks you. Has this beauty a father or a mother? You say she came to town to husband-hunt. She cannot have done that on her own.'

'No, indeed. She has no family, other than a mother who I gather is something of a recluse, her birth is dubious, and she is a companion to a pretty nonentity. To do her justice, she has caused the nonentity to blossom—another aspect of her damned perfection.'

'Jealousy,' said his sister quietly, coming over and giving him a gentle kiss on his cheek, 'is a very strong emotion when added to frustrated desire and the damage that wretched woman did to you. No wonder you look and sound so unhappy. Shall I order Chudleigh to fetch a barrel for you so that, like Diogenes, you may sit in it and hate all the world?'

'Oh, you are as bad as Pallas Athene. She is full of such learning. I often wonder how poor Chudleigh copes with you—he being so down to earth.'

'Oh, I have my quirks and he has his. Successful marriage consists in accepting one another's oddities with a wry smile and the ability to say, 'Precisely, darling,' in measured tones when one's other self says something mysterious.'

It was Nick's turn to kiss his sister's cheek when he had finished laughing at her sally. 'I had forgotten how much we were one another's other self when we were young. It's a great pity that we live so far apart. You have quite cured me of the megrims. The thing is, that if you ever met her, you would soon be bosom bows with Miss Athene Filmer.'

He was not being entirely truthful by claiming to

be cured, but if his distress over Athene was beginning to trouble his sister then he owed it to her and her husband to put on a better face which he did for the rest of his visit. Chudleigh's return from his fields put an end to their confidences, but not before Lucy had remarked, 'If you have fallen in love with her, Nick, then I can safely assume that she must be the sort of young woman of whom I would thoroughly approve—husband-hunter or not.'

Telling Adrian that she would not marry him was even harder than Athene had thought it might be.

He had come to see her when the week was up, his face shining with eagerness. He had half persuaded himself that little Miss Emma might be a better bet as a wife than her clever and beautiful companion, but when he entered the Tenisons' drawing-room to receive her decision he was struck all over again by Athene's classic beauty and her perfect composure.

It was, he thought—struck all poetical for once—like comparing fine wine with bread and milk, so serenely lovely was Athene beside Emma's more ordinary prettiness. The thought of making her his Countess, of seeing her presented at Court, of having other men envying him the possession of such a treasure, made him feel quite faint.

It did not occur to him that never once when he thought of her being his wife were the more earthy pleasures of marriage a consideration. Athene was to be a trophy as well as a bed-mate. Oh, he would bed

her, and she would give him his heir, but that was not
the main reason for her attracting him so much. He
was dimly aware that he lacked the intellect which
Nick and some of his friends and relatives possessed,
but by marrying Athene he would redress that bal-
ance. None of them would have a wife so beautiful,
so clever, so poised, so able always to say and to do
the right thing.

Alas, it had never occurred to him that she would
refuse him—and here she was, doing exactly that.

'But why?' he exclaimed, his honest face troubled.
'I thought that you liked me. I know that I like you,
love you, I mean,' he added hastily, dimly aware that
a stronger display of affection might suit him better
in the dire situation in which he had somehow arrived.

He had thought Athene's plea for delay mere girl-
ish nonsense: after all, girls were supposed to be un-
predictable, but that she might turn him down had
never entered his head.

'Oh, Adrian, I do like you, very much. But I like
you as a friend, not as a possible husband. Oh, I know
that you have so much to offer me beyond your own
kind self—wealth, position, a title, and a beautiful
home. In the end, however, there must be more than
that between us for marriage to be a possibility. No—
accept that, with the best will in the world, I cannot
accept your offer, and let us part as friends.'

'You are sure that you might not reconsider?
Would you not like a little more time?'

If Nick had not reproached her, if Mr Tenison had

not asked her to be true to herself, and most of all if her father had not told her of what he had endured because he had not been true to himself, Athene might have given way to spare Adrian the pain which he was obviously feeling. As it was, she could only think of the pain that a loveless marriage on her part might cause them both, and allow that to guide her judgement.

'No,' he suddenly said, reading her beautiful, troubled face correctly. 'I can see that that would not answer. Is there someone else, Athene, someone whom you could accept?'

At least she could answer that truthfully, remembering Nick flinging himself away from her, and her passionate denying response to him.

'No, Adrian, that is, not to say that there might not be someone in the future, but now, no, there is no one.'

'That's all right, then,' he said, relieved to learn that another fellow had not bested him. 'I told no one but Nick that I had offered for you, and I know that he left town without saying anything to anyone about it. I'm sure we both ought to keep mum; you know how odd society is about such things.'

'Yes,' agreed Athene, relieved. She stood to lose the most if it was bandied about that she and Adrian had secretly been discussing marriage and that she had, in effect, jilted him. Mr Tenison had told her that he had said nothing to his wife of Adrian's proposal to her. Mrs Tenison was unaware that Adrian had even visited the house on the fateful day on which he had consulted her husband before making his offer to Athene.

Mournfully Adrian bent over her hand.

'I can only wish you the best in the future,' he said. 'If you should decide to change your decision in the next few days,' he added hopefully, 'be sure to let me know on the instant. You have quite broken my heart, you know.'

He was being so kind in his simple-minded way that Athene felt her eyes fill with tears, but all the same she shook her head.

'No, Adrian, I shall not change my mind. And I wish you all the best, too.'

For good or ill it was over. Athene had refused the opportunity to become everything for which she had hoped and schemed before she had left Steep Ride, and when the door closed behind Adrian she was left with nothing but memories of what might have been.

Life had a nasty habit of going on, Athene discovered, as though the personal drama which had occupied her every moment during the last few weeks had not taken place. The sun rose and set. Balls were given, a boating party on the Thames took place, and the theatre was visited. In short, nothing seemed to have changed.

A few rumours made the rounds to the effect that young Kinloch no longer seemed to be smitten with the Tenisons' poor companion, and had stopped dancing attendance on her. No one was really surprised or interested in why he had. It was, after all, only to be expected, she was scarcely the right sort of *parti* for a titled young man of such great wealth and position.

Adrian flirted with a few girls, found them dull after Athene, and then, on an impulse, seeing the Tenisons and Athene seated alone at one of the greatest receptions of the Season, he went over to them. Yes, Emma *was* a pretty young thing, and since Athene showed no signs of changing her mind there could be little harm in keeping up his friendship with her.

'Oh, we have missed you lately, m'lord,' said Mrs Tenison cheerfully. 'Have you been out of town?'

'Oh, I've been otherwise engaged, madam,' he told her. 'I came to see if Miss Emma would stand up with me in the next dance.'

He purposely avoided looking at Athene—only offering her a distant bow—before walking off with her charge. Mr Tenison, who had already spoken to Athene about her refusal of Adrian, watched them go with a sad expression on his face.

When Athene had told him of her decision in the library, shortly after Adrian had left, he had said, 'I think that you are wise, my dear. You were not at all suited. Had you asked me to advise you, I would have told you that, and not because I think that now he has lost you he will offer for Emma, but because I care for your welfare. I can't oppose the marriage, even if I don't like the prospect of having a son-in-law whom

I can't talk to, but I know that she will be happy with him, happier than you would have been. My one worry is that you may have lost your best chance of marrying well.'

'No,' said Athene, remembering what her father had told her. 'I would not sell my soul in order to contract an essentially loveless marriage—even to gain the whole world—for the price might have been too high. Think only that you are the father I have never had, and that your kindness has made my life pleasant.'

They had parted after that, and now she was condemned, if that was the right word, to watch Adrian turn his attentions to Emma. His heart was not so broken, she thought wryly, that it was not mending itself in double-quick time! If he did intend to marry Emma, though, she wished them both well, even if her refusal of Adrian meant that she would now remain a spinster.

Nick grew increasingly restless in his Hampshire retreat. So restless that his sister's husband said to him over the port, one night at dinner, 'Old fellow, if this young woman you are mooning after is occupying you so much that Lucy is beginning to worry about your health, I suggest that you go back to town and have it out with her.'

So Lucy had told Chudleigh of Athene. Nick said solemnly, 'Does that come from the depths of your knowledge of human nature, Chudleigh?'

'No,' his brother-in-law returned, 'rather of that of the animals which surround us. They are more like us than we care to think. Make her, or break with her, but don't pine away like a ninny-noddy. Action is wanted here, not brooding.'

Nick lifted his glass in a mockery of a toast. 'Splendid,' he said. 'Action it will be—and if she is married, or pledged to be married to Adrian by the time I return, then I shall be off to Rosanna Knight's house on the instant, and bed either her, or her sister! Will that do?'

'Got it bad, hasn't he?' said Tom Chudleigh to his wife while they watched Nick's carriage drive away. 'Good fellow, your brother, but he don't take life easy, does he?'

It was a verdict which Nick was making about himself.

He arrived in London in the pouring rain, and for want of anything else to do visited Jackson's boxing saloon in Bond Street. Nothing much seemed to have changed in the month he had been away. There were the same fellows standing about, or exercising.

He was in the middle of lifting weights when he saw Adrian come in. He was looking singularly pleased with himself and the moment he saw Nick he mouthed something incomprehensible in his direction. Weight-lifting over, he rushed at Nick excitedly.

'Congratulate me, old fellow,' he exclaimed before Nick had so much as got his breath back. 'I'm to be married as soon as the lawyers have done their work, and I want you to stand up with me at the ceremony. I'm to be turned off at Kinloch House—it will hold more wedding guests than the Tenisons *pied à terre* in Chelsea.'

So soon! Athene—as she had promised at their last disastrous meeting—must have accepted Adrian shortly after his own retreat to the country. Everything was over, so he might as well stop mooning about the impossible, get royally drunk, and then bed Rosanna, or perhaps do it the other way round, as he had promised Tom Chudleigh. Before that, though, he had to say something to the beaming Adrian.

'I always believed that Athene would accept you,' he said despairingly. 'I suppose she thought that she'd look less mercenary if she held you off for a little.'

'Athene! Who said anything about Athene? No, it's Emma Tenison I'm marrying, dear little Emma, I can't think why I took so long to realise what a treasure she is.'

Nick gave a short, incredulous laugh. Could Adrian really be telling the truth? Had he, in a few short weeks, gone from adoring one charmer to adoring another?

'Well,' he finally achieved, 'that was a quick change of mind, and no mistake.'

'What's that? I didn't change *my* mind, Athene changed hers and refused me, and a good thing, too. We weren't really suited, you know. She was too clever for me—bound to have been trouble later on.

Whereas, my dear little Emma…' and he offered Nick a smile of such beaming fatuity that Nick could scarcely credit it—or what he had just heard.

'You mean that *she* turned you down?'

'Have you grown cloth ears in the country, old fellow? I've just told you that she refused me. Said that she liked me very much as a good friend, but marriage wasn't on. Said it would be a mistake… What's wrong with you, Nick, I've never known you so slow on the uptake before. Now, you'll forgive me if I toddle off. I'm taking my sweet Emma for a spin in my slow old curricle. I turned the new one over the other day practising for the race to Brighton, but the dear little thing's persuaded me to drop the notion. Said she wants me present at the wedding without a cracked head or a broken arm, and damme, she's right. As it was I sprained my wrist a little, and the curricle's done for!'

In the middle of the shock which Adrian's news about Athene had dealt him, Nick registered the comic fact that 'my sweet Emma' was already taking after her dominant mama and was ordering the so-called head of the family about!

And where was Athene while all this was going on? How did she feel about the rapid desertion of her recent squire, who had claimed to be so besotted by her?

Somehow Nick managed to offer Adrian some coherent congratulations, while mentally deciding that a rendezvous at Rosanna Knight's was not really on the cards now, but one with Athene at the Tenisons most definitely was. He dressed as quickly as he could and drove straight to Chelsea.

The only thing which he had to worry about was whether Athene had turned down Adrian in order to accept Inglesham!

He arrived at the Tenisons wondering what in the world he was going to say to her. To propose on the instant might be seen as being as equally abrupt and surprising as Adrian's immediate transfer of his affections from Athene to Emma—and what a turn-up that was.

He was still turning his tactics over in his mind when the butler, Pears, who had opened the door, informed him that Miss Athene Filmer was no longer in London.

'Not in London,' he echoed witlessly.

'No, sir. She has left us and I believe that she has returned to her home in Northamptonshire.'

'What is it, Pears?' asked Mr Tenison who had watched Nick arrive from an upstairs window and had immediately guessed what his errand might be, but thought it politic not to let Pears be aware of that when he appeared at the front door after an urgent and hasty run downstairs. 'Has Mr Cameron come to call on Miss Emma—or myself?'

'While I am always pleased to see you, sir,' returned Nick, bowing, 'it was really Miss Filmer I was hoping to see.'

'I think, sir,' said Mr Tenison, 'that it would be

better for us not to conduct business on the doorstep. Pray enter. Neither my wife nor my daughter are at home this afternoon, and I would be glad of your company as well as happy to enlighten you as to Miss Filmer's whereabouts.'

He led Nick to the room which served as his library and his study and offered him a glass of Madeira, which Nick, distractedly, took.

'I perhaps ought to explain,' Mr Tenison began, 'that my wife employed Miss Filmer to act as a companion to my daughter because she thought that she would find an older and more experienced one to be too oppressive. Miss Filmer carried out her task excellently, but after your cousin, Lord Kinloch, proposed to Emma, my wife was of the opinion that as she was shortly to be a married woman, Emma no longer needed her services. Accordingly Miss Filmer was asked to resign, which she did, and left Chelsea for her home, Datchet House, in Steep Ride, within the week. I am sure that you will find her there.'

He did not tell Nick of Mrs Tenison's indecent triumph after Adrian had proposed to and been accepted by Emma, nor that he knew of Adrian's proposal to Athene.

'I would have Filmer leave at once,' Mrs Tenison had told her husband. 'I think that she had some notion that she might snare Kinloch for herself, and I don't want her presence here to put a spoke in Emma's wheel.'

Mr Tenison could not assure his wife that she was

unlikely to do any such thing without breaching the confidence which Athene had asked for. He had been compelled to watch helplessly when his wife brusquely and summarily dismissed her.

If Nick thought that the whole business left a sour taste in both their mouths he did not say so. After all, his own conduct towards Athene had scarcely been blameless. He drank Mr Tenison's Madeira, thanked him for his information, chatted a few moments about current news—and left.

But not before Mr Tenison had said to him, 'I trust, Mr Cameron, that when you next see Miss Filmer you will convey my good wishes to her. I was sorry to see her go. She was a good hard-working young woman, and during her stay with us gave my Emma the confidence which she greatly needed and which she will take with her to her marriage to your cousin. May I, at the same time, offer you my best wishes for your own future.'

So the shrewd old fellow had grasped that he had been strongly attracted to Athene, and had let him know in his own inimitable fashion—and had wished him luck into the bargain!

Before she had left London Athene had visited Louise. This was easier than it had ever been before, since Mrs Tenison had relieved her of all her duties. 'I am not in the business of escorting her around the great houses of London so that she might try to catch another suitor now that she has failed with Kinloch,' being her unkind remark to her husband.

Louise heard Athene's news sympathetically. 'You are quite sure that you were wise to refuse Adrian?' being her only comment. 'From all that I hear of him he does not sound at all like my late husband. On the other hand the *on dit* is that he's a bit of an ass.'

'But kind,' agreed Athene. 'No, I have no regrets there. What in the world would I be able to say to him at breakfast after the excitements of the wedding were over!'

'True,' said Louise. 'When do you return to Steepwood, and how shall you bear missing the savour which living in London confers on life?'

'Oh, I have had far too much of that savour lately,' confessed Athene. 'I shall be happy to enjoy the leisurely delights of the country.'

'So you say now, but it might be a different matter when you're there. By the by, what about Kinloch's cousin—Nick something, wasn't it? Did you bid adieu to him as well as to Adrian?'

Athene answered her friend as carelessly and calmly as she could. 'Oh, he left London for the country some little time ago.'

'Did he, indeed? Was this before or after Adrian proposed, or you refused him?'

Athene had forgotten how shrewd Louise was behind her pretty, somewhat feather-headed appearance. 'Oh, my dear,' she finally achieved. 'We had the most tremendous set-to before he disappeared, and I'm sure that I shan't be seeing him again.'

Despite all her brave resolutions Athene's eyes filled with tears, and she could not stifle a sob.

'So, you did care for him. What went wrong?'

'Everything. He thinks me a cold conniving schemer who was after Adrian for his money and his title, and I only found out how strongly I was attracted to him after Adrian had begun to make a leg to me so determinedly and I was responding to him. Had I met him first—but there it was. He offered me nothing but reproaches, and I was equally harsh with him. The worst part of it all is that besides Mr Tenison, he was the only man I could talk to sensibly, and who talked back to me in the same vein—and he had to despise me for what he thought my venality. Oh, Louise, only someone like you knows how hard it is for a poor girl to make a life for herself in this cruel world.'

'Particularly,' said Louise dryly, 'when someone like Mr Nick Cameron, who has only known comfort and riches, can so cruelly judge those who have never owned them.'

'Precisely. Now let us talk of other things. Have you heard anything further about Sywell's death?'

'Nothing. I dare swear that you know more than I do, or that you might do when you are home again. You will write to me as often as you can, won't you? I shall miss you desperately. You are the one bosom bow I have, and as Nick Cameron was the only man to whom you could talk sensibly, so you are the only woman who performs that service for me! I will pray that you meet him again in better circumstances, although I cannot completely like someone who has been so unkind to you.'

The two young women embraced, and parted, Athene to finish packing, and Louise to return to the business of earning a successful living whilst praying that her true identity would remain a secret.

The one thing which sustained Athene on the drive back to Datchet House and Steep Ride and her mother, was that her mother would not be alone in the world as she had been since Athene's departure for London.

Her letter giving the news of her unexpected return arrived on the very morning that she did, and she found her mother waiting for her in the yard at the Angel, which was the post-house in Abbot Quincey. The sight of her drove Nick Cameron and everything which had happened to her since she had left home, out of her head.

'You look pale, my darling,' her mother exclaimed after they had kissed one another. 'Did London air not agree with you?'

'Oh, the journey was tiring, and yes, London is a dirty, smoky place, but very exciting, for all that.'

'Exactly as I remember it on my one short visit. I am surprised, if pleased, to have you home so soon—have the Tenisons not returned? I trust that you parted on good terms.'

'I will tell you everything in due course,' said Athene, who had no wish to begin informing her mother of her strange London odyssey in an inn yard.

'Indeed. Forgive my impatience, but I was a little troubled when I received your letter, and again when I saw you looking so poorly. Pure country air and food will do you the world of good, I'm sure.'

How small Datchet House now looked to one used to London's magnificence, how mean the streets in the villages they drove through, and how tiny the shops! Athene was shocked by her own response to the meagreness of country living. On the other hand the scenery was beautiful, and the water in the Steep River was clear and untainted when they drove by it.

Conversation was slow, too, she found, when neighbours came to call, wanting to know about the excitements of London and the Season. She had told her mother most of what had happened to her there, and while her mother understood why she had refused Adrian, she had grieved at the necessity for it.

'You would have been set up for life,' she sighed. 'Not left, like me, to pine alone in the rural fastnesses of country living.'

'But at what a price, Mother. You would not have had me pay it, I trust.'

'No, indeed. I understand you…but still…'

Athene said nothing of the Duke and his sad confession to her; consequently it was all the more surprising when, one afternoon, there was a knock on the front door, and their little maid being otherwise engaged, Athene answered it herself. Before her, on the doorstep, his handsome face anxious, stood the Duke of Inglesham.

'My dear Athene,' he said, somewhat surprised. 'I had not thought to find you here. I wonder if you would be so good as to ask your mother if she will receive me. I will quite understand if she feels that she cannot.'

'Of course I will receive you,' said Mrs Filmer from behind Athene's back. 'Even the most common criminal deserves a hearing, and you are far from being that.' .

She beckoned the Duke into the front parlour where Athene left them alone together: a pair of one-time lovers who had not seen one another for over twenty years.

Jackson had given Nick the Filmers' address in Steep Ride. He could not be sure how Athene would receive him—given the circumstances of their last meeting—but he readied himself for departure, hoping against hope while he did so.

He delayed setting off for a day when Adrian asked him to be sure to attend the reception which he was giving at Drummond House—his first. Mrs Tenison was acting as his hostess for this one occasion and was consequently on such high ropes that it was surprising that she did not float up into the air.

'You can't refuse, old fellow,' he pleaded. 'It'd

look damned odd if you cut line on my very first entertainment of the ton.'

Well, he could always leave early, but before he did so he was leaning against the wall, bored and weary, watching other people enjoying themselves, since London seemed stale to him now that it no longer contained Athene.

He remembered how pleasant it had been to be with her when he was not engaged in reproaching her. Her lively wit had informed all their conversation, and he could well believe Mr Tenison had been speaking the truth when he had said how much he would miss her.

Behind him two men whom he knew by sight had begun talking about the Duke of Inglesham.

'Surprised he isn't here,' said the first. 'Came out of his shell this year, didn't he? Probably gone back into it.'

'Oh, no. Tupman said that the rumour is he's dashed off into the country after one of this Season's beauties.'

'Good God, I thought he'd sworn off women after that shrew he married died. Which one is it he's after now—and why into the country?'

'Oh, his target is supposed to be nothing less than the pretty piece who used to stand behind the Northamptonshire heiress who's marrying our host. She left after Kinloch netted the heiress—not that she's that remarkably well endowed with tin, but she's pretty enough to make a good Countess. The heiress, I mean, not Inglesham's bit of muslin—the Duke surely can't mean to marry her.'

Nick's first instinct was to knock down the bastard who was slandering Athene, his second was to slander her himself by assuming that it *had* been the Duke that she was after.

On the other hand, he thought, when the two men had moved away, I can't necessarily assume that an overheard piece of gossip is true. I shall still go to Steep Ride as soon as possible and discover for myself whether Athene discarded the lesser to marry the greater. Yes, that's it.

Why in the world couldn't he have fallen in love with the dull and proper young woman whom every man of sense was supposed to wish for a wife? Chasing after a clever one might be seen as the act of a fool—or of a clever man! There was another thing to consider, too. It was time, as his sister had said reprovingly to him before he had left the Chudleighs, that he forgot the whole Flora Campbell business, accepted that not all women were like her and found himself a wife.

'And if it's the young thing over whom you've been pining, then I shall be only too happy to call her sister.'

And that was why, two days later, he found himself driving into Abbot Quincey determined to find out, once and for all, if he could start a new life, either without Athene, or best of all, with her.

If she would have him, that was.

* * *

Northamptonshire pleased him more than he had expected. One of Nick's friends had told him that it was dull, but then *his* notion of exciting scenery was the Swiss Alps, and after seeing them everything else must appear dull. He found Abbot Quincey to be a pretty little town, with a post-house, two inns and an alehouse outside which ragged old men sunned themselves in the warmth of late July.

Nick bespoke a room at the post-house when he discovered that Steep Ride did not possess an inn with lodgings. He left his chaise in the yard, his valet in the tap-room, and went for a short walk, turning over several strategies in his head before he drove to Datchet House. He had no notion of what sort of reception he might expect from Athene, but he thought ruefully that, given the cruel way in which he had behaved to her, it might be a harsh one.

He was on his way back to the post-house, whose proprietor had promised him nuncheon, shortly after noon, when he saw a handsome black coach being driven slowly towards him from the direction of Steep Ride. To his dismay, if not his surprise, he saw that it bore the Inglesham arms, decked out in red and gold, on its door, and that inside it was the Duke himself.

So, he—and the gossips—had been right. Athene had refused Adrian in order to hold out for Inglesham, and here he was, come to claim her. Or perhaps he had already claimed her.

Disappointment warring with anger, he was of half a mind to return to the post-house, eat his meal, cancel the rooms and return to London.

Chicken-hearted, he told himself furiously, you are chicken-hearted, and a fool beside. Suppose she has refused the Duke, what then? Would you lose her for nothing? At least I ought to confront her, discover what exactly her plans are, and if she is either the Duke's future wife or mistress, then, and only then, would a return to London not be the act of a coward afraid to confront an unpalatable truth—that I have, for the second time, fallen in hopeless love with a scheming mermaid. Lucy is right. I must face the future and forget the past: it has hung over me long enough.

Despite that brave resolution Nick never knew how he ate his nuncheon—nor could he have told anyone what he had eaten. He drank nothing but water, for he knew that he must keep his wits about him, and he drove to Steep Ride as slowly as he could, for he feared that to drive quickly would result in him speeding like a lunatic.

He had always prided himself on his cool command. He had always laughed at those who had run mad over a woman, and here he was, run mad himself. Whether it was his confused state of mind, a state he had never been in before, or whether time itself was playing tricks with him, he seemed to arrive at Steep Ride almost before he had left Abbot Quincey behind.

As he had been told, the place was little more than

a hamlet with one main street, so that Datchet House was soon found. He came to a stop before it, and alighted. It was modest, little more than a large cottage, with a garden before it full of flowers, and a porch framed in rambling roses before a door with a small glass window above an iron knocker.

Now, he would learn his fate. There was no going back.

Nick lifted the iron knocker and rapped the door twice. He was determined to be neither overbearing, nor timid. A classic calm must be his mode of conduct.

Athene was stitching a kneeler for the little chapel which stood at the end of the village street, where the curate came to preach on Sunday. Her mother, who was engaged in similar work, was talking about the Duke's return to her after they had spent so many years apart.

She was rosy-faced and happy, for once her first shock at the arrival of her lost lover was over she had been able to listen calmly to him when he had informed her why—at long last—he had come to see her.

'I find it difficult to believe,' she was telling Athene, 'that, after all these years, he still remembers me, and those few happy days which we spent together. Can I believe him when he tells me that he has never forgotten me, and that he wishes me to forgive him for having so cruelly deserted me, so that we may marry and give both you and me a name which can rightfully belong to us?'

'I think you can,' said Athene gently—she had said nothing to her mother of the Duke's approach to her before she had left London, for he had asked for that to be confidential, and it was for him to speak of it to her mother and not her.

She wondered how many more secrets she might yet need to keep, beside those of her friend Louise. She had told her mother nothing of her love for Nick and the unhappiness it had brought her because of her original determination to marry money and rank. She had, quite truthfully, simply explained to her mother that once Emma's marriage to Lord Kinloch had been arranged Mrs Tenison had decided that her services were no longer required.

She was sure that her mother would not have approved of her behaviour towards Adrian and Nick, and now that she was back home again she could not approve of it herself. Far better to let her mother enjoy her new-found happiness without troubling her with other people's miseries. The Duke had spent the morning with them discussing arrangements for his marriage to his lost love.

'I shall arrange for a special licence,' he had said, 'and a simple ceremony at the village church. I have had one grand marriage and it did not answer. This time I shall marry for love, not money. Besides, it will delay the gossip which will inevitably follow when I treat Athene as my daughter.'

Her mother had smiled agreement. The last thing which either she or the Duke wanted was to be the centre of all the excitement which a fashionable marriage in London would have inflicted on them.

'I still think that I am going to wake up and find that it is all a dream,' her mother was saying. 'Philip said that he would quite understand if I could not forgive him for deserting me, but I know only too well the kind of pressure which was brought to bear on him. The people I cannot forgive are my father and mother, who kept me from him and then turned me out, although I feel that I must inform them that I am finally to be married to the man I love.'

She gave a sad smile. 'I fear that they will forgive me when they receive my news and learn that I am to be a Duchess after all, but it will be too late for me to forgive them. Had they supported me, my dear Philip's father might have relented.'

It was at this point that there was the knock on the door and the arrival of the little maid to tell them that a Mr Nicholas Cameron had arrived asking if he might be allowed to speak to Miss Athene Filmer.

'Mr Cameron,' said her mother. 'Is that the young gentleman who is Lord Kinloch's cousin, Athene?'

Athene managed a 'Yes.' She had said virtually nothing about Nick to her mother, because every time she tried to talk about him she had the most desperate desire to cry. What in the world was he doing in Steep Ride? What could have occurred back in London to bring him here?

She was silent for so long that her mother said gently, 'Athene, the young man is waiting for an answer. Is there any reason why you do not wish to see him?'

'Yes…no,' choked Athene. Oh, why had she not told her mother the truth? She looked wildly around the pretty little room. She could not speak to him here, not among the memories of her happy childhood. Somewhere neutral would be better.

'Athene…?' prompted her mother a little anxiously. 'If you do not wish to speak to Mr Cameron you must tell him so at once. It is only courteous.'

'Oh, I will speak to him,' said Athene, summoning up all her courage. Supposing he had only come to reproach her again, what then? 'But I would prefer not to do it here. Do you think it possible that I could ask him to take a walk with me? I would feel happier talking to him in the open.'

'Possible,' said the bewildered Mrs Filmer, 'but a little odd. It would be more proper to receive him here…but if that is what you wish…'

'I do wish, and I will explain everything later on, when he has gone,' said Athene wildly. 'Would you be so kind as to ask him in, and talk to him while I fetch my bonnet and shawl?'

Odder and odder, thought her mother, after she had agreed and had watched Athene dash from the room as though her head were on fire. What sort of an ogre could Mr Nicholas Cameron be to inspire such trepidation, such agitation as she had never seen her usually composed daughter betray before?

Her surprise was even greater when the little maid ushered the young gentleman in. True, he was harsher of aspect than most young men were in these degenerate days, and his clothing was not that of a dandy. Nevertheless he had the face and manners of a clever man of the kind whom she thought Athene would enjoy being with.

Nick, for his part, took an immediate liking to Mrs Filmer and the modestly pretty room in which she received him. She was as beautiful as Athene, but, unlike her daughter, was small and gentle with a winning smile and an air of wishing to please and to conciliate. Her clothing, whilst not in the last stare of fashion, was designed to suit a widow who had retired to live in a country village.

'I hope,' he began after he had introduced himself and Mrs Filmer had assured him that Athene would receive him shortly, 'that I have not arrived at an inconvenient time. If so, I will leave and call later.'

He didn't wish to do so in the least, but for some reason, Athene's mother aroused all his protective instincts. He wondered what the unknown father must have been like from whom Athene must have inherited her intellect and her determination.

'Oh, no,' she reassured him. 'My daughter was speaking of taking a walk, and it might be an excellent notion for her to show you the village where we have spent so many years.'

Nick solemnly agreed, and tried to hide his impatience until the door opened and Athene arrived—at last. He was sure that for her own reasons she was delaying seeing him as long as possible.

Although her blue dress, shawl and bonnet were as modest as her mother's turn-out, they suited her. She was a little pale, perhaps, but her manner was as calm as ever. Perhaps it was that which set him wishing that he could take her in his arms and tell her that he loved her. Common-sense, and the memory of Inglesham's carriage, told him that he had no notion of what she had been doing and deciding since he had last seen her a month ago.

He bowed, and came out with, 'Athene, I mean Miss Filmer, you look as well as ever.'

Good God, was that the best that he could do? But the presence of her mother and Athene's frozen propriety—even though she had suggested a *tête à tête* walk for the pair of them—seemed to have ushered him in the direction of the North Pole, too!

'Thank you, Mr Cameron,' she responded coolly, 'you appear to be in the best of health, also. I trust that you left Lord Kinloch and Emma in excellent fettle.'

'Very much so. Preparing for the wedding and hoping that you might be present when it comes off.'

'That might be difficult to arrange,' she said gravely. 'I understand that you wish to speak to me. I believe that our meeting might be a more fruitful one if we undertook it on neutral ground as it were.

I shall, therefore, be happy to show you Steep Ride and its immediate environs.'

Nick bowed again. 'And I shall be happy to see them.'

What a ridiculous conversation, thought all three participants at one and the same time. Athene's inward comment was that an observer might think that they were engaged in writing their own book of etiquette, so proper and grand were they being.

Nick bowed to Mrs Filmer, and made his only completely truthful remark of the afternoon so far by saying, 'Very happy to have met you, Mrs Filmer.'

'And I you,' said Athene's mother. What she was really thinking was, Goodness, what on earth have these two young people been getting up to so that they are unable to speak naturally to one another in front of a third party?

Outside, in the open, watched by a nearby cat and two distant waddling ducks, and no one else at all, Nick took Athene's arm in his and walked her away from Datchet House and towards the wooded country which lay beyond the end of the village street.

She was the first to speak when the rough road degenerated into a track and they were out of sight of possible curious eyes. 'Why are you here, Mr Cameron? What is your purpose in pursuing me?'

He swung her gently around so that she faced him, before forgetting everything he had told himself about decorum, about being gentle with her, to fire at her as though she were the enemy—the memory of seeing the Duke in his coach informing every word he uttered—'Is it Inglesham, then? Did you refuse Adrian so that you might marry him? If you object to me following you here, I suppose that he received a different welcome.'

Dazed, Athene stared at him. She genuinely had no idea why Nick should reproach her about Inglesham. She knew that he had said earlier that he suspected her of dangling after the Duke, but that memory had been obliterated once she had discovered that Inglesham was her father.

'Inglesham!' she exclaimed, and then, horror of horrors, she began to laugh, nervous laughter which had no mirth in it. 'You think that *Inglesham* has come here to propose to me? Did you follow him here, too?'

'No, but I saw him in Abbot Quincey this morning, coming from Steep Ride. Why, Athene, why?'

His face was as tormented as Athene felt that hers must be. She suddenly took pity on him—who had had so little pity for her, but she could not resist teasing him a little…

'Is it your opinion, then, that the conduct of a father is reprehensible if he takes an interest in his daughter?'

Nick stared at her in astonishment. 'Of course I agree to that, but what has it got to do with us?'

She gave him her sweetest smile. 'Oh, Nick—' Mr Cameron had disappeared '—the Duke is not my suitor. And he never has been. He is my father, the father of whom I had no knowledge until shortly before you left London for the country. He has come to Steep Ride, at long last, to marry my mother. I cannot tell you their story—that is for them to do. You have tormented yourself for nothing.'

'Inglesham?' Nick stammered at her, all his usual self-possession deserting him when he grasped what a monstrous mistake he had made. '*Inglesham* is your father?'

'I have just informed you so, have I not? As usual you chose to believe the worst of me. Now leave me alone and allow me to return home.'

She began to walk briskly up the road away from him, so that he might not see that her tears were about to fall, for the self-control on which she had always prided herself was deserting her—so much so that instead of walking back towards the village she was rapidly making her way into the woods near Steep Ride, and not away from them.

Such stupidity, she was raging to herself; he has turned me into a watering-pot with his folly. He is a very Othello to think me always in the wrong. First he was jealous of Adrian, and with some justice, and now it is the Duke, with none. Next, it will be the Prince Regent, or the Shah of Persia, or perhaps the Emperor Alexander himself—even the Angel Gabriel is not safe.

Nick watched her retreating from him. Inglesham was her father, not her lover, and he, in his blindness, had tormented himself and reproached her because he had not possessed the decency to understand that she had renounced Adrian for the best of motives and not because she was greedy for even greater wealth and position than he possessed.

He had been a fool, once, twice, thrice a fool, and now he was going to lose her, the only woman with whom he had ever been able to talk as freely as he would with one of his fellows. A woman whom he had first lusted after and now loved. To make matters worse, with the Duke's patronage and the dowry he would certainly give her she might have anyone she wanted, anyone at all, and, dammit, the only anyone she ought to want was himself.

He began to run after her, heedless of who might see him, for he must immediately try to repair his jealous folly before he lost her for ever. He caught her up where she stood hesitant, realising that she had gone the wrong way. Nick was panting, not with haste, but with the shock of learning the truth. He could not lose her, nay, he must not lose her.

'Athene,' he said hoarsely, detaining her with a look rather than trying to check her physically, 'Athene, can you ever forgive me? I think that I have been madly in love with you ever since I first met you, so that when you seemed to prefer Adrian to me I was in a ferment of jealousy. I was wrong to reproach you for being mercenary and running after him...'

'No,' said his contrary mistress to this confession. 'No, you were right at the time. At first, I *did* run after him, because he was just the sort of jolly and kind fellow who was lucky enough to possess wealth and a title as well—someone whom I could safely marry without loving him. And then when I got to know *you*, I began to change my mind, and something my father told me made me renounce Adrian because I didn't truly love him and it would be wrong to marry him. But it was too late, wasn't it? You had made up your mind about me.'

Nick thought that she was about to run away from him again.

'No, don't go,' he said hoarsely. 'Forgive me if you can. However badly I have behaved towards you, I have always loved you. There it is, the truth, out at last.'

Before he could stop himself, he took her in his arms: whatever else, he could kiss away the tears which had begun to run down her cheeks.

'Oh, Athene,' he sighed. 'I have dreamed of doing this ever since the first time I first saw you, standing behind young Emma,' and he began to kiss her, gently at first and then with increasing passion.

At first Athene let him hold her, let him kiss her tears away, without responding to him. And then, as his passion grew the greater, hers flowered into life, and when he kissed her on the lips, she returned his kiss so enthusiastically that it was Nick who pulled away with a sigh, fearful of where their mutual transports were leading them.

Transfixed, Athene stood back and stared at him

before saying, 'I thought that you despised me, not loved me. When did this remarkable transformation take place? How, loving me, could you think that I would behave in such a two-faced manner?'

'Jealousy,' he said simply, putting out a hand to stroke her warm cheek. 'And the memory of what happened to me when I first loved a woman whole-heartedly. She deserted me for a richer man shortly before the wedding ceremony, and in my misery and stupidity—for that is what it was—I have been suspicious of all women ever since. To be fair, you must admit that the whole Inglesham business only seemed to make sense if, knowing nothing of his relationship with your mother, one were to assume that he was after you.'

'Well, he was,' said Athene uncontrovertibly, putting her hand over his, 'but not in the manner in which you thought. He had no children by his first wife and he wanted to reclaim the daughter he had lost years ago. Goodness, from the way in which we have all been going on we might have been enacting one of Shakespeare's lesser plays.'

'*The Comedy of Errors,* perhaps,' said Nick, regaining his sense of humour once his jealousy had flown out of the window. 'And now there is nothing left for me to do but ask you if you can forgive me enough to agree to marry me.'

'Could you believe that I am not sure how to answer you? Even if I love you, which I most demonstrably do, will it be possible for me to be happy with

a husband who will run mad if I look at another man?
Dare I take that chance?'

'Could *you* believe that I have learned my lesson
and will trust you in future? My mother once told me
that I was a conceited boy who thought that I knew
the answer to everything. Since I met you I seem to
have had the answer to nothing. You're sure that you
won't regret not marrying Adrian, or possibly someone even grander—someone like your father?'

'No,' said Athene simply. 'I don't want to marry
any man because he is grand. I want to marry someone I love for himself, and that man is you.'

'Is that a yes or a no?'

'Yes, it's a yes. I have to believe that you mean
what you say, and that we can deal as happily together as we have done so often in conversation and
in play whenever we forgot that we were at odds with
one another.'

'That we were at odds was mostly my fault,' he
told her sorrowfully. 'I don't deserve you. I misjudged you, and for that I apologise to my darling
Pallas.'

'There is no need for you to apologise, for I, too,
was at fault from the moment I arrived in London. I
misjudged myself in thinking that I could marry without love—and so I left myself open to be misjudged
by you.'

'Nevertheless,' he said, taking her in his arms
again, 'perhaps this will convince you that my apology comes from the heart.'

This time she responded to his kisses so fiercely from the very beginning, that again, in order to resist temptation, he had after a time to pull himself away with a groan.

'It must be the woods which are affecting us,' he said, looking around him. 'Did you really mean to run into them? Were you looking for your owl for advice, my lovely Pallas? I would have thought that you would have run into safety—not away from it. They are tempting me to do that which must wait for our wedding if we are not to be forsworn in church!'

'I scarcely knew what I was doing when I ran from you,' she said. 'Perhaps the woods were kind for once and lured me into them so that you might follow me where no one could disturb us. The legend says that they are unkind to strangers and those who would desecrate the Abbey, hence the violent deaths of so many of its recent owners. Perhaps they do not see me as a stranger, since I have roved freely in them all my life.'

Nick answered her with a restrained kiss before saying. 'You may be right, but they are dark and stern enough to support any story of death and tragedy. Today, however, they must bear witness to the merry tale of lovers finding themselves at last. I cannot wait to introduce you to my parents and to my dear sister, Lucy. They were fearful that I would never marry, and here I am, caught at last by a very witch who has freed me from the foul enchantments of the past.'

'And Scotland,' said Athene merrily. 'Don't forget

Scotland. You must take me there, for I have never been farther north than Northampton and I can't wait to see "Caledonia, stern and wild…", the land of Sir Walter Scott.'

'I have every intention of taking you there once we are safely married—and that as soon as it can be arranged—we have lost too much time already. And now we must return to Steep Ride in order to show your mother that I meant you no harm. She gave me what my nurse used to call an old-fashioned look when I invaded your parlour—and no wonder, I must have appeared beside myself!'

Hand in hand they walked back to Datchet House, where they found the Duke's carriage still standing outside it as proof that not one, but two pairs of lovers had, in the end, found what all men and women hope for, their other self, with whom they might achieve happiness and fulfilment in the future.

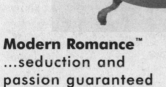

Modern Romance™
...seduction and
passion guaranteed

Tender Romance™
...love affairs that
last a lifetime

Sensual Romance™
...sassy, sexy and
seductive

Blaze.
...sultry days and
steamy nights

Medical Romance™
...medical drama on
the pulse

Historical Romance™
...rich, vivid and
passionate

29 new titles every month.

*With all kinds of Romance for
every kind of mood...*

MILLS & BOON®

Makes any time special™

MAT4

MILLS & BOON

ALWAYS
DAKOTA
Debbie Macomber
NEW YORK TIMES BESTSELLING AUTHOR

Matt Eiler has a wife who doesn't believe he loves
her and an old flame intent on causing trouble –
will it be for better, for worse…for always?

Available 16th November

*Available at branches of WH Smith,
Tesco, Martins, Borders, Eason, Sainsbury's,
and most good paperback bookshops.*